It was the worst assignment of Kate Diamond's career. Worse than the time she had to jump over a snake pit. Worse than the time she had to steal a ruby from an ice hotel and definitely worse than the time she toppled into a volcano.

Why? Because of one person. Ace Mason. In a quirky twist of fate, her ex-FBI partner and ex-boyfriend was now her new partner at the Ritzholdt Museum. Their assignment is to pose as a newly rich married couple on board their private luxury yacht to ferret out the famous international art thief, The Lemur. Too bad the mission is plagued with problems including a cast of quirky suspects and the troublesome fact that Kate and Ace have to share a room.

Lucky thing Kate has the help of her retired jewel thief parents and their band of thieves, safecrackers, and con men from the Golden Capers retirement village because everyone on board the yacht is suspicious. But while Kate is busy scrutinizing the suspects and dodging Ace's attempts to reconcile, The Lemur is busy crafting a clever misdirection that could ruin all of Kate's well-laid plans.

D1529021

HEIST SOCIETY

Kate Diamond Adventure Series Book 3

LEIGHANN DOBBS

This is a work of fiction. None of it is real. All names, places, and events are products of the author's imagination. Any resemblance to real names, places, or events are purely coincidental, and should not be construed as being real.

Chapter One

It was the worst assignment of Kate Diamond's career. Worse than the time she had to jump over a snake pit. Worse than the time she had to steal a ruby from an ice hotel. And definitely worse than the time she was pushed into a volcano.

But it wasn't the assignment so much as the person she was assigned to do it *with:* Ace Mason. The man who was posing as her husband was downright irritating. Never mind that his cocky attitude was somehow charming. They had a history, and Kate wasn't about to fall into that trap again, even if the assignment included posing as Ace's wife.

Standing beside him on the deck of the luxury yacht The Leviathan, Kate did her best to ignore Ace as she glanced over the railing and listened to the ocean lap lazily against the side of the boat. Sun shone down and highlighted the beauty of Vis Island and the pristine, white sand beaches of Gradac. Coming from her somewhat unorthodox background, she'd never imagined Croatia was such a beautiful, tropical place.

Then again, she'd never imagined being fired from her Federal Bureau of Investigation job either. That had been due to the man at her side—the reason for the irritation, and for the grudge she continued to nurse. It had been the reason for their breakup as well. But that was old news. Kate was her own person now, and the last thing she needed was another man telling her what to do, even if it was only for show.

"You hungry?" Ace asked, glancing over at her. "The brunch buffet's ready, and we really should mingle with our guests."

See? It was starting already. Give the guy a fake title of husband and he assumed he was her boss. She gave Ace a supremely annoyed stare. It really was unfair that he should look so good in his disguise — navy blazer, crisp white linen slacks, and aviator shades. Heck, even his fake mustache added an air of debonair danger.

She, on the other hand, felt like a reject from Gilligan's Island, with her stuffed bra and crazy bouffant red wig, her fake eyelashes sticking out to there and her bubblegum-pink lip gloss that was sticky and saccharine sweet—not her usual style at all. She much preferred jeans and T-shirts, or comfortable clothes she could move around in easily. All the better to catch some criminal in action.

But they were on a mission for the Ritzholdt Museum. To add insult to the injury of their past, the museum had hired Ace to work as her partner. There was no getting out of it—and Kate had tried. She was stuck, but she didn't want to let her boss, Max, down. So she went along with it. For now.

Kate turned slowly, unable to resist getting in a slight dig on her former FBI partner and ex-boyfriend. She even gave Ace a little salute, though not quite the one they taught in the military—more the one-fingered style, with a distinct emphasis on a certain finger. "Aye aye, captain."

"I'm not playing the captain this mission. That honor falls on your pal Benny. I'm just your ever-doting husband." Ace exhaled slowly, as if Kate were a petulant child he was forced to contend with, and flashed her a tight smile as he took her elbow and tugged her forward, none too gently. He raised his voice and added a tinge of southern accent. "This way, Pookie."

Kate scowled at him. He'd been teasing her with his ridiculous pet names, saying it was good for their cover, but she refused to play along. Somehow pet names made it seem as if they were very close. And they weren't. Nor were they going to get any closer on this trip, despite the way they had to act.

She slid her huge sunglasses over her eyes and pinkie waved to several of the assembled glitterati as they made their way under the overhang into the shade and the waiting buffet table laden with every imaginable kind of fruit and seafood, in addition to a full array of breakfast favorites. There were the regular scrambled eggs and bacon, of course. But that fare soon gave way to more decadent treats like lobster toast and caviar jam.

Kate had to say that when her boss, Maximillian Forbes, set out to pull a sting operation on a crook he spared no expense. In truth, this whole overnight journey to Venice was nothing but an elaborate ruse to catch the infamous art thief the media dubbed The Lemur. All of the guests on board the yacht now were suspects. She and Ace were the bait.

Well, not them exactly, but the rare painting rumored to be in their possession. Max had spread the news far and wide that Roger and Connie Carlson — the married, country-bumpkin couple she and Ace were playing in this farce — had purchased this artwork on the black market with no idea it was actually a rare treasure stolen by the Nazis that everyone had thought had been destroyed by Hitler before the fall of the Third Reich. If such a thing actually existed, it would be priceless. As it was, they only needed The Lemur to *believe* the painting existed and try to steal it so they could catch him.

The cruise was supposed to be a high-society event put on by Roger and Connie to solidify their prominence in the art world. The final day, a reception was planned at which Roger and Connie were to present Max with a rare painting for the Ritzholdt. Not the fake painting, of course, Roger and Connie were smart enough not to show that one off. They had it stored safely away on the ship.

Too bad Max wasn't on the trip. That would make it much more interesting. But he was as evasive as usual, planning to meet them in Venice for the reception. Oh well, at least then Kate would finally be able to see him face-to-face. Would he look as good as he sounded? That hardly seemed possible, but Kate couldn't wait to find out.

"Smile, sweetheart," Ace whispered near her ear, dragging her from her thoughts. For a second she thought that Ace sounded just as good as Max. Probably just the acoustics here inside the yacht. "We're supposed to be happy newlyweds," Ace hissed. "We used to be happy together. Remember?"

The slight sadness in his tone tugged at her heart. Trouble was, she did remember, all too well. Even more so after the end of their last case had resulted in a steamy kiss that still set her lips tingling whenever she thought of it, which was entirely too often. But he'd gotten her fired from the Bureau, ending the career she'd worked so hard to build. If that didn't cool a gal's ardor, Kate didn't know what did. Even though a few years had passed, she was still too angry and hurt to even begin contemplating forgiveness of his sins.

She shook her head and stepped away from him, her best fake grin firmly in place. "Yes, baby. You just make me so happy I want to pinch you. Hard."

"Didn't know you like the rough stuff, but whatever floats your boat, honey." Ace winked, and darn if those fresh butterflies didn't swarm in her stomach. Seemed no matter how angry she was with him, he could still set her heart whirling. Blasted man! If she had her way she'd push him overboard and set about catching The Lemur herself just to prove she was still the best at her job. And better than Ace could ever hope to be.

As Kate moved along the line of delicacies, she inconspicuously watched the people around her while pretending to focus on filling her plate. Ahead at the buffet table stood suspects number one and two: Sinclair Robinson and his wife, Feisty.

Now there was a misnomer if ever there was one. Feisty Robinson was about as timid as they came, so afraid of her own shadow she rarely left her stateroom. Probably a good thing too, because her husband had a terrible reputation as a womanizer and couldn't seem to keep his hands off any passing female. Kate had to wonder if his sticky fingers pertained to more than the opposite sex. She'd caught Sinclair downstairs earlier, nosing around in the yacht's storage area where the fake painting was held in a safe.

Of course, the minute he noticed her Sinclair feigned ignorance and claimed to be lost. Was he using his groping ways to cover his criminal activities? Perhaps he used his wife's supposed agoraphobia and chronic illnesses as an excuse to avoid suspicion and gain sympathy. Looking at Feisty Robinson now, Kate believed she looked healthy enough, if not a tad pale. She made a mental note to keep an eye on the couple.

Kate stopped near Uncle Benny at the end of the

table and looked over their guests. "Should be an interesting trip."

"You can say that again," Benny said, looking past Kate. He wasn't really her uncle, just a member of her parents' old crew from Golden Capers Retirement Community, an ex-security hacker who'd gone by the name of Bangkok Benny in his heyday.

"My, my," a sticky sweet female voice said from behind Kate, making her hackles rise. "I wondered where all the handsome men had gone."

Kate glanced sideways to see another guest, Alexis Pennington — mid-forties, widow, wind-tunnel look from too much Botox and plastic surgery, at least in Kate's opinion — all but wedging herself between Kate and Benny, which was no easy feat considering Benny's considerable girth. Kate had to admit, though, that the crisp captain's uniform of white slacks and navy blazer suited him well, as did the jaunty captain's hat on his head.

Benny, along with all the Golden Capers gang — Kate's parents, Carlotta and Vic Diamond, Gertie Rosenblume, and Sal Munch — were along for the cruise, all posing as members of the crew to help catch The Lemur.

Kate felt safer with all of them around, despite their backgrounds of a certain "questionable" nature.

She'd grown up around these people and trusted them with her life. Far more than she trusted Ace these days. After the stunt he'd pulled, showing up in Mexico and acting as though he'd saved the day — even though he did, she supposed — but that didn't make up for how he'd spilled his guts to the FBI about her infractions in handling things. Well, enough was enough.

And yes, Ace had apologized a million times and denied knowing Kate would end up losing her position with the Bureau over it, but what had he expected when he'd told them she hadn't followed agency protocol? Did he think they'd buy her candy and flowers and promote her to head of the Bureau?

It had worked out okay in the end. If she hadn't been fired from the FBI, she wouldn't have this great job at the Ritzholdt. And she did truly love her job. Going undercover to retrieve artwork that had been stolen from the museum or procure rare objects was a lot of fun. It was a thrill to pull off a heist and know you'd never be arrested because no one in their right mind would report that someone walked off with an item they'd previously stolen. And even if she did get into trouble, Max always got her out.

A thin smile spread across Kate's face. It was poetic justice that her last job for the Ritzholdt was what had ended Ace's FBI career. It served Ace right they'd fired his butt too. He'd gone AWOL to come down to Mexico because he thought she was in danger.

Danger, schmanger. He'd done it to show off, end of story. That was the real reason behind his actions, and she knew it. Then he had the gall to turn around now and claim he wanted her back. Well, fat chance buddy. He'd have to do a lot more groveling and proving himself before that could ever happen.

"Have any of you seen my Aunt Dottie?" Alexis asked, looking genuinely distressed. "I can't seem to find her, and I like to keep an eye on her, poor thing. I think she's starting to get a little … ." Alexis twirled her finger around her temple in the universal sign for losing it and then batted her eyelashes up at Benny.

"I saw her out on the deck earlier." Benny stepped back from Alexis, who was sidling closer to him.

Considering Benny was old enough to be her father and a bit on the rotund side, Kate wondered about the attraction. Was she really interested in him, or was getting in good with the captain a way for her to gain access to areas of the ship that might otherwise be off-limits to passengers? Alexis took a firm slot on Kate's suspect board.

Kate studied Alexis. According to the dossier Max

had put together, Alexis didn't have much money. Though she dressed in expensive clothing and took expensive trips, word on the street was that it was all paid for by her elderly aunt. She'd been a guest at several parties where The Lemur had struck. Maybe Alexis was The Lemur carrying out her thievery under the guise of accompanying her aunt?

"I say, this food is excellent." Sinclair and Feisty appeared with loaded plates. Sinclair stood next to Benny, their navy blazers almost a perfect match except for the captain's insignia on Benny's shoulders. Appropriate that Alexis and Sinclair should be standing together, given their apparent proclivity for flirting. Maybe the two of them would get together.

Alexis moved closer to Benny. Or maybe Alexis preferred men in uniform.

As Kate struggled to think up something clever that Connie might say, the lights flickered and the yacht lurched sideways. Alexis stumbled into Benny full force as Feisty's plate clattered to the floor. Sinclair dropped his plate right before ramming into the other side of Alexis, sending them all flying into Kate.

They stumbled for a few seconds before the lights flickered on and the ship steadied, but not before Sinclair managed to grab Kate's butt.

Kate held back from whacking him, and patted her hair. Hopefully the wig hadn't gone astray.

"Oh dear, I am so sorry!" Feisty's hands flew to her cheeks as she looked down at the food and broken dishes strewn on the deck.

"No worries," Kate moved to Feisty's side, glad to have an excuse to get away from Sinclair. "The staff will clean it all up. Bless their hearts. Now you go and fill up fresh plates."

Benny coughed and straightened his tie. "Sorry, folks. This is a new ship and we have a few kinks to work out. I do believe that was the docking crew casting off. We're ready to get underway, so if you'll excuse me ..." He headed toward the bridge, leaving an obviously disappointed Alexis behind.

"My apologies for that little bump." Ace stood in the middle of the crowd. "I guess these new boats prefer to be treated with a more gentle touch. Like my lovely wife."

Everyone laughed as Kate plastered on a smile and tried to act enamored with Ace. Gertie and Sal rushed around picking up the mess on the deck.

"Still plenty of food left." Ace gestured toward the buffet, which had escaped the lurch unscathed.

Alexis still stared after Benny with a lovesick expression. "Where did the captain say he saw Aunt

Dottie again? I do hope she wasn't hurt when the ship almost capsized just now."

"For God's sake," Ned Parsons said from the main salon. He stood a few feet away, but paid close attention to their conversation, apparently. His wife Cindy, another mousy woman who'd barely said two words since boarding the yacht, stood at Ned's side, looking infinitely embarrassed by her husband's rudeness. "Really, Alexis, the ship did not almost capsize. And you must keep better watch over your aunt. We're now at sea. Mind she doesn't fall overboard."

As if in answer, a drunken snort rang out. Kate and the others leaned over to see Dorothy Mayhew, better known as Aunt Dottie, sitting at the bar talking to Sal. A tall, thin bottle of Stoliano liquor sat on the bar next to her, and Sal tipped it into her tumbler, pouring only a few drops over the ice. The octogenarian seemed perfectly content to hit the sauce and joke with their pretend bartender. She looked nothing like her niece, with white hair, jolly blue eyes, and a sweetly wrinkled face that made one want to hug her and have her bake Tollhouse cookies.

"Ah, well. I guess I'd better check on her then," Alexis said, peeling away from the group.

She gave a jazz-finger wave and floated off, leaving a cloud of cloying perfume in her wake. Kate pulled a face and Ace chuckled, handing her a freshly filled plate and tucking his arm around her waist to lead her to a table near the railing. Kate did her best to keep her smile plastered on and not shake off his touch.

Ace, of course, seemed both amused and delighted by their married-couple identity. And why wouldn't he? This all probably fit right into his plan of wooing her back.

She tried to squirm away, but he pulled her even tighter, an amused smile quirking his lips. He was actually enjoying this! Kate bet he wouldn't like it so much if she stomped on his foot to get him to loosen his hold. But she couldn't do that. She had to keep up appearances for the sake of the mission.

"What was that with the lights and the ship lurching?" Kate spoke in low tones so no one would overhear as she smiled at the guests filling fresh plates.

"Inexperienced crew," Ace murmured. "Takes a while to get the hang of things."

"I just hope that doesn't happen for the entire trip."

Soon they were gliding out of the Gradac harbor into the open sea, on their way to Venice. Crystal-clear turquoise waters surrounded them, salt spiced the air, gulls screeched, and the scene seemed idyllic.

Well, except for the whole stolen Nazi art thief on the loose thing. Max had even upped the ante, spreading the rumor that the painting was an unknown Picasso. Max figured this combination of forbidden fruit hidden in the safe below deck would be irresistible to The Lemur.

For Max, this catch was personal. The Lemur had stolen numerous artworks over the years, including several from the Ritzholdt Museum. He wanted them back and he wanted The Lemur behind bars. Kate intended to make sure that happened.

"Luxury suits you, honey bear," Ace said, watching Kate over the rim of his juice glass, his expression a bit too smug for her liking. What she wouldn't give to reach over and rip that fake mustache right off his lip. See how he liked that. "You should try it more often."

"And maybe you should … ." She caught herself before finishing the sentence. Instead, Kate reminded herself they were undercover as two lovebirds, and held her tongue—and her reach—keeping her voice low. "Who's your top suspect so far?"

"Hmm." Ace devoured a couple bites of scrambled eggs with cheese and vegetables as he surveyed their small contingent of guests. "Honestly, no one yet. I don't know them well enough. Nearly every one of them seems suspicious. Take Ned Parsons. I've caught him twice now studying the paintings Max hung in the main salon. He seems far more interested in them than a routine connoisseur would. And speaking of those paintings, where did Max get them all? I can't imagine he'd pilfer his own museum for them, but then again I can't imagine Gertie would have time to forge them all."

"I'm not sure. Max has connections we can't even imagine. I mean, somehow he came up with a whole yacht for us. A few paintings is nothing." Kate watched Ace over the rim of her coffee cup as he nibbled his toast, his short, dark hair gleaming in the sunshine. She looked away. "And yeah, I can't see Gertie making all those either."

Funny, she hadn't really realized Gertie had such a hidden talent. Back when she'd been part of her parents' circle of criminals, Gertie had always acted as a safecracker on their heists. Tall, slim, somewhat Hispanic-looking, Gertie had always been like an aunt to Kate growing up. She was mouthy and opinionated, and told the best dirty jokes.

"Ned's on my radar too," Kate said, refocusing on the case. "Max obviously thinks he's suspicious, which is why he and his wife Cindy were invited. Apparently, Ned has somehow managed to turn up at several of the same Ritzholdt Museum functions where a piece of the museum's collection has been stolen. Could be coincidence, but Max doesn't believe so. He said museum security has caught Ned snooping around the private offices several times."

"Interesting," Ace said, finishing his breakfast and then pushing his plate away. As he crossed his arms, Kate did her best not to notice the way his crisp blue polo clung to his muscled chest and shoulders. "What do you make of Penny Martin and her husband, Lawrence? For a married couple, they don't seem to pay much attention to each other. In fact, she seems far more interested in watching us."

Kate had noticed that too. Raised by a pair of former cat burglars, Kate was sensitive to being the object of staring. Penny Martin always seemed to have an eye on her. They kept bumping into each other too, as if Penny was following Kate. It made no sense at all.

Why would Penny trail after country-bumpkin Connie Conway, when she was supposedly newly married? At least that's what Max had put in her file. She'd also been overheard at various functions making inquiries about rare artifacts, and had asked about several items that had been stolen from museums over the years, wanting to know if they'd turned up or if the investigations had uncovered any new information.

If Penny were The Lemur, though, why would she ask about the items? Wouldn't that draw attention? The questions she'd asked made it sound as though she were hunting for information as to whether the authorities had a lead on the thefts. If she were behind the thefts, this might be a way to get information so she could cover her tracks.

Now that Ace had pointed out the strange vibe between Penny and Lawrence, Kate did find it odd. As she watched, Lawrence got up and walked away from Penny at their table without even a glance or word to his wife. He went to stand near Alexis at the railing, flirting shamelessly with her. Penny didn't seem to care. She was too busy staring at Ace and Kate, as usual.

"Well, lucky them if they'd rather be apart," Kate said, just to get a jab in at Ace.

Then, at his arch look, she sighed. "I'm not really sure what to think of them either. I've bumped into her a few times since we boarded, but I haven't really had a chance to get a handle on her. And Lawrence looks far more interested in the rest of the women on board than he does his wife. If this is their second honeymoon, then I'm Vanna White."

"I'd like to buy a vowel please." Ace chuckled at her flat look. "It was a joke." He sat back and exhaled slowly, scrubbing a hand over his face. "Well, I think our best bet for now is to keep an eye on everyone. And watch that painting downstairs. My guess is if The Lemur's on board, and Max seems certain he is, he'll want to scope out the area below decks first, see the best hiding places and ascertain where the art is stored. I'd wager the best time to stage a robbery would be tomorrow night, after we dock in Venice. That's when the big final reception takes place, and we're supposed to present the painting to Max for his museum. Everyone will be at the reception, so The Lemur will have a perfect opportunity to take the painting out of the storage room and slip off the boat."

"And if he — or she — is smart, they'll want to figure out exactly where that painting is while we are at sea so they don't waste time hunting for it during the party," Kate said.

Ace nodded. "Then it's a simple matter of slipping into the room, grabbing it, and making a discreet exit."

"Good thing Max installed those cameras in the hallways downstairs between the guest suites so we can keep an eye on things remotely." Kate sipped her mimosa and gazed back at the lovely island they'd just left, all white sand beaches and ancient stone buildings. Such an odd and fascinating contrast. She wouldn't mind returning to Croatia on vacation to do some real exploring. In fact, if it wasn't for the mission and the mess between her and Ace, this was a dream trip come true. Luxurious yacht, gorgeous scenery, excellent food — even if her present company left something to be desired.

As Kate shifted in her seat, her legs brushed against Ace's beneath the table. A wave of annoying memories washed over her. When they'd been a couple and partners at the FBI they'd been good together. She'd seen a future with him, maybe even forever.

Then he'd had to go and screw it all up. Her warm, fuzzy feelings toward Ace were squashed under an avalanche of anger. If there was anything the Diamond family prized it was loyalty. You didn't betray those close to you. Ever. Ace had broken that cardinal rule, and she wasn't sure she could ever trust him again. Not professionally and not personally, and certainly not with her battered heart. And even though her parents had seemed to forgive him and her father was taking a shine to the man, Kate didn't share those feelings.

Kate fussed with the sleeve of her flouncy peach silk chiffon bathing suit cover-up and glanced up at the tinted window of the yacht's bridge to see Benny gesturing through the glass for her attention. She cocked her head toward Ace and pushed her empty plate away. She'd been right. The food had been scrumptious. "I think Benny wants to see us."

"Looks like break time's over," Ace said, staring up at the bridge.

"Yep." Kate affixed her best affectionate smile as Ace slid his arm around her waist and they checked in with all their guests before climbing the stairs to the second-deck bridge. "Time to get back to work."

Chapter Two

"What do you mean the camera's not working?" Kate frowned and fanned herself, glad to be out of the hot sun. It was one thing when you were in normal clothes, but with a heavy wig and full makeup, the heat made her itchy and irritable.

Benny waved them over once Ace closed the door. The bridge was smaller than Kate would have thought, but set high on the boat, so the view was spectacular. Sparkling turquoise ocean stretched for miles beyond the harbor they were now navigating through. Gulls flew high in the powder-blue sky, their wings bleached stark white where the sun hit them. Their muted cries could be heard even through the thick glass. A large sailboat glided across the horizon.

Having Benny pose as captain on this journey had

been another surprise for Kate, but Max had insisted Benny knew what he was doing around a yacht. Apparently Benny had served a stint in the Merchant Marines in his youth, and that's where he'd earned his old nickname, Bangkok Benny, after a particularly raucous shore leave in Thailand. Growing up, Kate didn't remember him ever talking about his past or where he'd gotten his name. Not that any of the pasts of any of the residents of Golden Capers Retirement Community came up often, unless it regarded comical aspects of their criminal exploits.

"Look at this." Benny pointed at a laptop that sat atop the control panel. Or was it called a cockpit? It looked state of the art, with gleaming stainless steel, crisp white fiberglass, and rich mahogany details. Dozens of dials and small navigation screens dotted the surface.

The laptop showed the feed from the small camera they'd placed in the storage room. Unfortunately, its screen was blank.

"See that?" Benny jabbed his finger at the screen. "No feed at all. It's wireless, but I've already checked the connections and run remote diagnostics on the receiver from here, and both are fine. That means it has to be the camera that's malfunctioning."

"Perfect." Ace's tone suggested it was anything

but. He sighed and peered out into the harbor ahead of them. "How long until we're in open waters?"

"Not long," Benny said. "Maybe half an hour or so. Why?"

"Guests are starting to roam, get more comfortable. The Lemur could take an opportunity to do a bit of snooping around the ship." Kate looked out the windows. The Adriatic looked so peaceful and serene. Hard to believe they were sailing with a bunch of suspects who'd probably just as soon shoot someone as get caught stealing a black-market masterpiece. "Fine. If you can tell me how to fix the camera, I'll go down there and repair it now before we miss something important."

Benny frowned. "It's one of Gideon's gizmos, and you know what that means."

"Complicated," Ace said.

Gideon Crenshaw worked for the Ritzholdt as the museum's gadgets expert. He was always coming up with gizmos and gadgets that would help them on their missions. He was also responsible for the disguises like the one Kate was wearing that was digging into her and causing her to itch. She made a mental note to get back at him for that. The thing was, Gideon's contraptions were usually overly complicated.

"Anyway, I think the key to that tiny camera is the itty bitty spring that Gideon installed between the processor and the small battery. My guess is something happened to that spring. Open it up and make sure the spring is situated between the red switch and the battery. If it's not that, check the switch. The battery should be fresh. I put it in myself yesterday."

Benny had barely finished giving Kate the instructions when a knock sounded on the bridge door. Ace and Kate exchanged a look, and Benny closed the laptop. Alexis Pennington entered without waiting for a response. Her flowing tie-dyed caftan billowed in the breeze, carrying with it the scent of salt, sand, and expensive perfume. She had her gaze trained on Benny alone as she wafted forward into the bridge. Her smile looked positively predatory.

"There you are, captain. You promised to show me your equipment." Alexis sidled up to Benny, letting her double-entendre hang heavy in the room, and Kate bit back a laugh. Benny's face flushed and his eyes widened. He looked a bit scared in the face of such blatant seduction.

"Oh, and I brought you a little something I wrote, captain." Alexis reached inside the deep V-neck of her caftan, between her breasts, and pulled out a piece of thick stationary, the edges embossed in gold.

"It's nothing really, just a short poem about romance on board." Her smile turned sly. "All hands on deck, captain, if you know what I mean."

Ace coughed to cover his inappropriate chuckle and failed miserably. Kate nudged him in the side and tilted her head toward the door. "We'll give you two some privacy."

Kate ignored Benny's imploring look as she steered Ace outside and down the stairs. "Well, at least somebody's having fun on this trip."

"We could have fun too. If you'd loosen up a bit." Ace glanced sideways at her. "When are you going to forgive me?"

"Maybe never, if you keep asking me about it," Kate said.

They reached the deck then veered left into the open salon. Ned stood against the far wall, staring at a painting on the wall. Near the stairs leading below decks were their final two guests, Sinclair Robinson and his wife, Feisty.

Kate glanced over and caught Ace's eye. He nodded. One good thing that had survived their former partnership was the shorthand communication between them. They could convey volumes with only a nod or a simple gesture.

After a smile toward Ned, who barely seemed to

notice anyone or anything other than the artwork, Kate and Ace headed downstairs. Just as they made it to the hallway, the ship lurched right, knocking Kate and Ace into the wall. From the galley behind them the sounds of plates smashing and glasses breaking echoed through the air, mixed with startled gasps from Carlotta — Kate's mother and their chef for this short voyage.

"Okay, Pookie?" Ace asked, straightening from where he'd huddled around Kate during their stumble into the wall. He put his hands on her shoulders, his gray eyes registering genuine concern.

"I'm fine," Kate snapped, more harshly than she'd intended. She stepped away from him, annoyed with herself for the prickle of awareness spiking through her from his nearness. "And you don't have to call me pet names when other people aren't around. I'm not your girlfriend anymore."

He looked at her and frowned, hurt and disappointment flickering through his eyes before he turned away. "My mistake."

From one of the rooms at the other end of the hallway came a feminine shriek and a masculine curse — Sinclair and Feisty, Kate presumed.

"Alexis must've gotten to Benny up on the bridge,

or the ship has some issues," Kate said as she walked the hall.

"Yeah, let's hope it doesn't sink," Ace said, his gaze narrowed as he kept pace beside her. "Let's find this camera and get it fixed so we can get out of here. I don't like it down here. Too cramped for my taste."

Considering he was six-four and built like a Greek god, Kate imagined just about anywhere except the outdoors would feel confining to Ace. She rushed after him, not wanting to give him the lead, only to stop again as the galley door flew open and Carlotta stepped into the hall, looking decidedly flustered, most likely from having her kitchen destroyed by Benny's carelessness. She arched a dark brow at Ace, the silver strands in her brunette hair glimmering beneath the overhead recessed lighting. "Mr. Carlson, could I see you in the galley a moment please?"

Carlotta Diamond would not take kindly to having her wares scattered willy-nilly. Kate bit back a grin at the spark of anger in her mother's deep-brown, almond-shaped eyes. Though she was nearing seventy, she still looked like an Italian starlet from the sixties. Her mother even spoke with a hint of an Italian accent, which was perfect for her role as chef this go-around. Kate took more after her father Vic in coloring, with her coppery red hair and amber eyes. Still, none of this made the situation any less intimidating to poor Ace, if the wary look on his face was any indication.

"Best get in there, Mister Carlson." Kate laughed and smacked him on the back as he slunk off toward the galley and her waiting mother. "Don't worry, I'll make sure things are tidied up out here and the store-room is secure."

She continued down to where the camera was located at an intersection of two hallways. Below decks on the yacht was like a maze, with several tight hallways crisscrossing and tiny rooms used for storage or for the crew's quarters. It was well lit, but the absence of other people made it seem a bit creepy to Kate. Then again, having no one else around to see what she was doing was a plus.

She paused at the door to make sure no one had followed, then turned the knob. Locked. Crap! Ace had the key in his pocket.

Not about to let that stop her, Kate plucked a bobby pin from her bouffant and picked the lock in seconds. Lock picking was a skill she'd learned from the Golden Capers gang at an early age, and it often came in handy. She slipped inside the dark room and closed the door. Fumbling for the light switch, she clicked it on, then squinted at the shelf across from the storage box where the forged painting was secured.

The tiny camera hidden inside the base of an empty can of furniture polish reminded Kate of the one they'd hidden in a brooch on the Lowenstaff case — a previous mission she'd gone on for the Ritzholdt. Those were the days. Back then Kate worked solo. She'd been fully in charge, with no partner to mess up the works. Ace had meddled in that case too, but at least he hadn't been working for the Ritzholdt at the time.

She unscrewed the canister and shook the camera into her palm to check the spring and battery as Benny had instructed, but before she could pry it open the handle on the door behind her jiggled.

Heart pounding with adrenaline, Kate shoved the tiny camera into her bra just as Sinclair Robinson strolled in. What was it with guests not waiting to be invited on this mission? He stood, one foot in the room and one in the hallway, seemingly as shocked to see her as she was him.

"Uh, is there something I can help you with, Mr. Robinson?" Kate asked, doing her best to keep her voice steady and her smile sincere. "It's easy to get lost in this maze of corridors."

"Me? Oh, no. I'm not lost, my dear. Not in the

least." A predatory smile bloomed on his face and he stepped fully into the tiny room, closing the door behind him and forcing Kate to back up a step to avoid standing chest to chest with him. "I must say, you look lovely in that frock, Connie."

His lascivious gaze roved over her, suddenly making Kate long for a bleach shower. She was still undercover, though, and continued playing her part, placing a fluttering hand on her chest, partially covering the deep V-neck of her salmon-pink maxi-dress. If circumstances were different, she would've punched him in the face and asked questions later. Creep. She tinted her voice with a bit of southern accent. "Why, Mr. Robinson, thank you for noticing."

"Of course. I am a connoisseur of beautiful things, my dear. And you are certainly exquisite." He moved closer, invading her personal space even further. It took all of Kate's training and willpower not to knee him in the groin. "Am I out in left field if I suggest perhaps you came down here hoping to meet me?"

Yes. "Well, I simply can't say." Kate bolstered her plastic smile by batting her fake eyelashes. Flirting wasn't her thing, so she prayed she was doing it right and looked enticing and not like an idiot with something in her eye.

He reached out and traced the tip of his finger down her bare arm. She suppressed a revolted shudder. This was so not what she needed to be dealing with right now.

"Too bad we weren't all alone when the ship lurched a moment ago. The way you fell against me I could have held you tighter ... and longer ... and all sorts of interesting conclusions could have followed." Sinclair was practically panting.

"Uh, yeah. That would be lovely, but I should, um, really get back upstairs now. The other guests will be wondering what's happened, and I wouldn't want to appear rude. My Roger will wonder where I've been. You remember Roger? Big, muscled guy. Could deadlift about three-fifty easily?"

She sidled away and tried to reach the door, but it was a miscalculation on her part, Kate realized too late. Her move only brought them closer together, allowing Sinclair to really get his hands on her. He seemed to have morphed into an octopus, touching everywhere. Kate struggled to get away from him in the tight confines without doing him serious bodily damage.

Not that she wouldn't enjoy that right about now, but she was supposed to be a country bumpkin, not a well-trained former FBI agent. She opened her mouth to call for help when the door jerked open and Ace crowded inside, taking in the scene with an ominous scowl.

"Everything all right in here?" he asked, his voice edged with steel.

Sinclair immediately released her, and Kate almost fell into Ace. She was never more relieved to see him than she was right now, though she would never admit that. "Yes, yes. Everything's fine. I was just giving Mr. Robinson a tour of the below-deck area."

"Right." Ace's polite smile was at direct odds with his frigid stare as he tucked Kate under his arm. "Well, then. If you're finished, Skrunky Unkims, we should attend to our other guests. I'm sure Sinclair can find something else to occupy his time."

"Of course, of course." Sinclair looked like a fish out of water, blotchy faced and gasping. "I appreciate your consideration, Mrs. Carlson."

He gave a little bow toward Kate. She clenched her fist to keep from punching him in the jaw. But he was still a suspect, and Max would not be happy to hear she'd decked him until they had proof of his guilt or innocence.

After he left, Kate pushed away and made a face at Ace. "Skrunky Unkims?"

Ace shrugged, clearly amused. "Come on, the pet names are part of the act. You should use them too. It's fun."

"I bet." Kate pushed past him out into the hallway.

"Come on, admit it. You were glad I rescued you in there."

"Hardly. I can take care of myself. I just didn't want to knee him for fear it would jeopardize the mission." Did Ace really think she needed to be rescued? She'd show him. She picked up the pace, and he trotted along behind her.

"Did you get the camera fixed?" he asked.

"No." Kate stopped in a deserted part of the hallway and reached into the front of her dress to fish out the camera still lodged there. "I got it out from the can, but didn't have a chance to do anything with it before Mr. Handsy interrupted me. I'll take it up to Benny and he can check it out himself. He can put it back too, once it's fixed. I don't fancy getting trapped in that storage room with anyone again."

"Good plan."

They started walking again. The fresh ocean breeze at the top of the stairs seemed fresh and inviting compared to having to breathe in Sinclair's stale breath in the storage room. Kate took the steps two at a time, then stopped at the railing and stared at the waves rushing past the bow of the ship. Based on the yacht's speed, they seemed to be making good time now.

"I still can't figure out what Sinclair was doing down there. He gave me some story about putting his wife down for a nap, but I don't buy it. She's a grown woman." Kate crossed her arms and narrowed her gaze. "I think we should find out what Sinclair was really doing down there, because judging by the surprise on his face when he walked into that room, he was definitely going there for a reason. Either he was expecting someone — or some thing — to be there, and it definitely wasn't me."

Chapter Three

Kate and Ace didn't meet up again until after lunch, when they gathered with the other members of the Golden Capers team in their private suite.

Kate had returned to their suite earlier and showered to remove the thick makeup and her wig so her scalp could breathe again. Plus, she'd wanted to wash away any lingering traces of Sinclair's unwanted pawing. Afterward, she stretched on her end of the luxurious cream leather sofa, propping her elbow against the back cushion and resting her head in her hand as she listened to her old friends banter. Of course she'd have to put her costume back on again later for dinner, but she didn't want to think about that now.

Gertie toed off her orthopedic shoes and propped her feet on the contemporary glass-and-steel coffee table in front of her Minotti navy mohair chair with a relieved sigh. Her gray maid's uniform did little for her olive-skinned Mediterranean complexion. "Lucky for you two lovebirds Max was kind enough to rent a yacht with a king-sized bed, eh?"

"How could you possibly know about the bed?" Kate asked, feeling testy. "And Ace and I aren't lovebirds."

"Hmm. Well, being the pretend maid has its advantages." Gertie winked and took a long swig of her white wine spritzer. "Besides, you know I see and hear everything."

"Really?" Ace rolled his eyes and flopped down on the other end of the sofa from Kate. "If that was the case, you should've noticed right away that I'm sleeping here on the couch for the duration of the mission."

"I'm surprised my father didn't get with Max to plan this whole fake marriage thing anyway." Kate rubbed her sore temples and gave Ace a look. "He thinks he's so clever."

"Speaking of clever," Ace said, shifting his attention to Benny. "I wonder what caused that ship malfunction earlier."

"Like I said, it was the dockhands. One of them pulled up the chain too quick and that jerked the ship." Bennie shrugged. "That's why I ran up to the bridge when I did. No harm, no foul. Dealt with worse in the Merchant Marines."

Ace raised a brow. "That was the first time. What about the second time?"

Benny turned as bright scarlet as the chair he sat in. "Hey, I can't help it if I'm irresistible to the ladies. There's more of me to love."

"Hey, Romeo." Sal crossed his arms over his chest and smirked at Benny. "I know you've been busy messing around with the suspects, but did you get a chance to fix the camera? It's critical to our objective. You do remember what that is, don't you?"

Benny flushed a deeper red. "I remember the objective. I couldn't fix the camera, though." He fished around in his pocket and tossed two halves of a tiny, rusted broken spring onto the table. "The metal on this is so thin and the sea air so corrosive that it rusted right through. It's no good, and without it the camera won't work."

Gertie leaned forward and picked up the spring. "Huh. Imagine this tiny little thing could mess up our whole mission." She tossed it back and looked at Kate. "I'm sure Gideon gave you some spares, right? I mean it's not as if we can go out to Walmart."

"He must have." Kate got up and went into the bedroom, returning with a bag of gizmos their tech guy had given her before they'd boarded the yacht. "There's a lot more than springs in here. Let's see what goodies he gave us this time."

It was always a surprise to see what gadgets they had to play with on a mission, and this time was no exception. The first thing Kate pulled out was a small black velvet box that contained two somewhat gaudy rings with wide gold bands and a large red stone. There was also a note from Gideon, which she read aloud. "These bands are actually a secret notification system. The stones are buttons you can press to send a radio signal to the other ring, which will vibrate, sort of like the handheld reservation alert devices restaurants use."

Carlotta raised a perfect brow at the rings. "Not my style for sure."

"Yeah but it *is* Connie and Roger's style." Gertie slipped one of the rings on long enough to admire it, then pulled it off and tossed it on the table. "What else you got in there?"

Kate pulled out the next set of objects — cut-glass whiskey tumblers and a bottle of clear liquid.

"Now we're talking." Gertie eyed the glasses.

Kate squinted at the tag attached to the top of the bottle in Gideon's scrawl. "Invisible dye. Will glow purple when seen through the bottom of these cocktail glasses. Note the glasses must be activated by alcohol first and will only work for thirty minutes afterward."

"Sounds interesting." Vic picked up the bottle to study it.

"Next we have ... ." Kate reached back into her bag of goodies and pulled out a pair of five-inch stilettos covered in rhinestones, a matching bracelet, and stud earrings.

"I'm guessing those aren't for me." Ace chuckled. "At least I hope not.

"Well, that'd be a whole different kind of mission then, eh?" Carlotta winked from her seat next to Vic at the dining table.

Kate's toes ached just looking at the precarious shoes, but at least they'd match the elaborate gown she'd chosen for the reception the following night. Kate set them on the floor and read the attached note from Gideon. "The shoes have removable heels in case you need to run after a suspect." Well, that was something at least, she supposed.

"The bracelet." She picked up the shimmering

wide cuff paved with rhinestones. "Has a map of Venice on the underside. And the earrings contain a GPS tracking device. All I have to do is click the back, and Benny can track me from the bridge anywhere within a hundred-mile radius."

Overall, Gideon had gone a bit overboard on tech this time, at least in Kate's estimation. Given the short duration of the mission and the fact they were all trapped on the ship together, she doubted they'd really need any of his gadgets. She hoped they'd figure out the identity of The Lemur well before they docked in Venice tomorrow night. She grabbed one of the stilettos again and turned the sparkling shoe this way and that, admiring the rainbow crystal reflections. At least Gideon seemed to have an eye for fashion.

"What else is in that bag?" Benny asked.

"Not much." Kate reached into her bag once more. "Looks like all that's left is more makeup and false eyelashes and a replacement wig for me, in case anything happened to the first one." She turned the empty bag upside down and shook. "No spring."

"Damn," Ace said. "That means we won't have the advantage of video surveillance to catch The Lemur in the act."

"Maybe we can call Gideon and have him heli-copter out a replacement," Sal suggested.

"Good idea." Ace stretched out on the sofa. "I'll give him a call. I think he forgot a few other things too."

"Like what?" Vic asked.

Ace gestured toward the pile. "He didn't put anything in there for his number one spy."

Kate couldn't help rolling her eyes. "Oh, he did. Look at all the stuff he gave me."

Ace shook his head and put his phone on speaker and set it on the coffee table so they all could hear. Kate put away her gadgets and leaned forward as the call was picked up.

"Ritzholdt Museum, Mr. Forbes's office," Mercedes LaChance said in her usual chipper, busi-ness-like, irritating tone. Okay, so maybe it was only irritating to Kate, but still. The petite brunette with her perfect diction and perfect nose always seemed to keep Kate from actually seeing her mysterious boss, Maximillian Forbes. Kate had been working for him for two years, but all she knew about the head of the museum was that he couldn't position a camera worth a damn and he had the sexiest accent she'd ever heard.

"Hi, Mercedes. It's Ace Mason. We were hoping to talk with Gideon, if he's available."

"I'm sorry," Mercedes said, not missing a beat. "Mr. Crenshaw is on vacation at present. Is there something I can help you with?"

Kate sighed, glad they weren't on Skype. "We need a tiny spring for the camera Gideon sent us. Oh … and Ace thinks Gideon forgot to give him some gadgets."

"I see. Give me a moment please." The sound of drawers being opened and closed mingled with the yips and barks of Gideon's little dachshund, Daisy. Mercedes must be watching the dog while he was away. "No. I'm sorry. I don't see any small springs. Or anything for Ace."

"Did Gideon leave a number where we could reach him?" Kate asked, giving Ace a superior look. "In case of emergencies?"

"Aren't you going to be out of communication range soon?" Mercedes asked, the frown in her voice evident. "I know for a fact Mr. Forbes had a jamming device installed on board The Leviathan before you set sail that's set to jam all communications from the ship to the mainland after you reach international waters in the Adriatic. He wanted to be sure The

Lemur and his accomplices couldn't transfer information with any associates off the ship."

Kate wanted to answer with a snarky retort that nobody liked a know-it-all, but Ace intervened. "Yes, I knew about that. It's why I brought my satellite phone. No cell service or Wi-Fi necessary. Wouldn't do to have all of our communication channels severed, would it?"

His affable manner seemed to charm the normally no-nonsense Mercedes, and the woman actually giggled into the phone. That earned another hard eye roll from Kate. "Yes, Mr. Mason, I suppose that's true. And aren't you the smart one for thinking of it too."

That last bit earned an even more exaggerated eye roll and a sour face. Smart one, indeed.

"Thank you, Mercy." Ace gave Kate another smug look, and she sat on her feet to keep from kicking him hard in the shin for using that woman's pet name. "But I'll be sure to use the excuse that we're too far out to sea to receive adequate cell communication if any of the other guests ask."

"Wonderful." Mercedes all but purred, and Kate's hackles rose. Not because she was jealous. Why would she be? She and Ace had gone their separate ways.

Who he flirted with was his business, even if his choices left something to be desired.

"I've been on cruises in the area where you are, and believe me, the communication is spotty at best, even with a high-tech satellite phone," Mercedes said. "Must be the distance or the atmosphere or something. Nothing but static and crackle until it all just fades away."

Kate wished this phone call would turn to static and fade away, but she kept her opinions to herself as Ace and Mercedes chatted amicably for a few more minutes before he finally ended the call.

"So, guess if we need to make any important calls we best get them done soon," Benny said. "And we need to figure out how best to use the gadgets Gideon gave us."

"Well, I say we use this invisible dye as another way to monitor who comes and goes from that storage room. I had to pick the lock to get in there earlier and it was far too easy." Kate picked up one of the tumblers and turned it in her hand, then looked up to find the rest of the group watching her closely. Everyone except Ace. She gave a dismissive wave. "It's a long story, but Ace had the key and we were separated and — oh, never mind. Anyway, we can coat the inside of the locks on the door and the safe with this liquid. Maybe even put a dab on the edges of Gertie's fake painting as well. If The Lemur tries to get in there, we'll know about it." She sat back and crossed her arms. "Ace and I can then use the cocktail glasses at the party tonight to see if anyone's been marked. Maybe we won't need that camera after all."

"You'll only have thirty minutes, though, right?" Gertie asked. "You'll have to make sure you time things accordingly."

"No, it's only the glasses that work for thirty minutes at a time. The dye will stay active indefinitely. We used something similar on a job years ago," Vic said, reaching over to grab the little bottle from Kate. "I'll spread the dye as soon as I get back. And Sal, don't forget to drop some hints about something secret and valuable in the storeroom while you are pouring those drinks behind the bar. I can work on maintenance things below decks, unobtrusively, and keep an eye on who's coming and going. We can compare notes later to make sure we don't miss anyone."

"Sounds great, Dad." Kate picked up the black velvet box containing the rings and handed the larger one to Ace. "Here. In case we get separated tonight and need to get each other's attention."

"Aw." He took it and slipped it onto his finger. "And here I didn't think you cared."

"I don't." She took hers out of the box, ignoring the stab of pain and regret in her chest. Before Kate could slip her ring on, Ace took it from her and grasped her hand, sliding the ring into place on her left third finger, right next to her fake wedding band. Her breath caught and her eyes met his, and for a moment time seemed to slow. Warmth and sadness and some other emotions Kate couldn't quite define mixed in his stormy gray eyes. "Well, Smoochums, call me crazy, but I still do."

Ahs and coos filled the suite as the rest of the team dispersed.

Kate cleared her throat and pulled away, suddenly self-conscious. "Yeah, well good thing this is all pretend. Fake marriage, fake relationship."

"Yeah, good thing," Ace said softly. He pushed to his feet, his expression unreadable. "Why don't you stay down here and rest a little longer? I'll go back up on deck and schmooze. You can come up later."

Kate sighed as the door clicked shut behind him. There he went being all sweet and nice again, making her want to forgive him even though her common sense told her he acted that way with everyone. Ace was just a nice guy. Period. But sometimes just being nice wasn't enough.

Besides, she'd moved on, put him and their relationship behind her.

So why, then, was her heart still fluttering from his whispered confession of still caring?

***

ACE WALKED back upstairs onto the deck, hiding his emotions behind a bland, polite smile. Most of the guests were milling about before dinner, dressed to the nines, but all he could think about was the exchange he'd just had with Kate below deck.

He'd not really meant to go there, with the fake rings and all, but something about holding her hand and saying those words got to him. She did that to him. Got him all riled up and discombobulated, and next thing he knew he was making an idiot out of himself.

He strolled to the railing to stare out at the crystal-blue sea, white frothy waves churning as The Leviathan sliced through the water. The ship was lovely. Not as lovely as the woman downstairs, but close. He sighed and stared down at the Adriatic.

Truth was, he never should've gone down to

Mexico the way he had. In the end, it had cost them both everything and torn them apart. Not that he was sorry he'd helped Kate. He'd never be sorry about that. Hell, he'd go AWOL one thousand times over for her if that's what it took.

But his interference had only served to anger Kate. She'd taken it as a betrayal, as some kind of sign that he didn't think she was competent or capable at her job. Which couldn't have been further from the truth. He admired Kate more than any other agent in the biz.

"Lovely evening," Penny Martin said, moving in beside Ace at the railing. "Thank you for inviting me, Mr. Conway."

Ace gave a curt nod and turned slightly to look over the gathering guests. "Where's your husband tonight, Ms. Martin?"

"Oh, Lawrence is still napping downstairs," she said, not meeting his gaze. "And please, call me Penny."

"Sure thing. If you'll call me Roger." Ace gave her a small smile, the one the ladies seemed to like. He wasn't above flirting with a suspect if it led him closer to his ultimate quarry. "Well, may I say you look pretty tonight?"

Penny blushed and glanced away from him, her

short dark hair blowing in the breeze. She was no Kate, but Penny was cute in a teacher-ish sort of way. From the prim, proper gown — not too revealing, not too loud or tight or memorable — to the tips of her sensible pumps, she seemed a bit out of place with the other guests. And there was the way she always watched Kate.

"Where's your wife, Roger?" Penny asked, bringing their conversation around to her favorite subject again. "Must be hard, coming from such humble beginnings as you and Connie did, to all this wealth. Tell me again how you and your wife came into your sudden fortune?"

Yep. There was that suspicion again. Ace cleared his throat. "Well, we won a lottery. Mega Ball Challenge in Tennessee. Cleared a huge sum after all the taxes were taken out. Quite a few million." Lucky thing Max had arranged things so that if anyone researched the story they'd discover that Roger and Connie had indeed won the Mega Ball. Never mind that it wasn't actually a real lottery; only the most diligent of research would uncover that fact.

"And you decided to invest in art?" she asked, a slight edge to her tone. "Without knowing the market or anything? That might not have been a wise move.

The art world can be quite cutthroat. Lots of thieves just waiting to bilk you for all you're worth."

Ace gave her a side glance at that. "We're just simple country folk who believe in the kindness of people. We like supporting the arts. Plus, I heard it was a good investment. But who would want to take advantage of us?"

"One never knows." Penny smiled, the sentiment not quite reaching her cool brown eyes. "I do hope you have the right insurance."

"Always." Ace decided to turn the tables on her. "And I hear you are quite an art connoisseur. Maybe you could help us with some of our acquisitions. Do you work for a gallery?"

"Hardly. Lawrence makes enough on his stocks and bonds to support us." She crossed her arms. "I've always been interested in art. If I hadn't married Lawrence, I think I might have gotten my degree and maybe painted myself."

"Oh, so you paint?" Ace asked.

Penny shrugged. "A bit. It's a lovely pastime."

Lawrence emerged at the top of the stairs, Alexis Pennington draped on his arm like a trophy. Ace narrowed his gaze at Penny, searching for some reaction. Even the most well-adjusted couples still felt twinges of jealousy. But there was nothing. His instincts told him something wasn't right with that relationship, and he made a mental note to check into it later.

Kate had followed Lawrence Martin up the stairs, and she now stood at the top of the steps. His heart stumbled, as it always did upon seeing her. Even in that ridiculous costume and all that makeup, she was still the most gorgeous thing he'd ever seen.

"Uh, if you'll excuse me, Penny. My wife's arrived." He took off without waiting for her reply, his attention focused solely on Kate.

Chapter Four

By the time the dinner buffet was ready, Kate was mingling with the rest of the guests on deck. Ace had been oddly clingy since his strange pronouncement in their suite when he'd slipped the fake ring on her finger, and she was glad for some time alone to catch her breath.

As she stood at the railing looking out at the aqua water rushing past and the last few Adriatic bottlenose dolphins still playing in the wake churned up by the yacht's engines, she couldn't help wondering about the significance of Ace's words. As hurt as she'd been by his betrayal, their relationship before those last final days had been good. Really good. So good, in fact, that she'd started to fantasize about them actually tying the knot one day. But then life and circumstances had intervened, and here they were now, polite associates, nothing more.

Except those few seconds in their suite when he'd held her hand and slid that ring on her finger and gazed into her eyes with an expression of both sadness and hope, and no small portion of longing, the connection between them hadn't felt polite. It had felt raw and real and incredibly right.

And that's what worried her the most.

She'd been burned by love and by Ace once before. It had nearly killed her.

Could she possibly open her heart and trust him again?

Maybe.

"Blast it all," Ned Parsons said from a few feet away. Seemed he'd finally taken a break from staring at the art in the salon. He was an odd duck, dressed more like a college professor than a member of the aristocratic European family from which he was supposedly descended. "I can't get any reception on my phone." He glanced around at the rest of the guests and raised his voice a few notches. "Can anyone get a signal out here?"

A hushed murmur ran through the guests as everyone pulled out their devices and checked them. Kate stifled a smile and looked over to catch Ace's eye. He winked and hoisted his glass in a small toast. Seemed they'd passed that point Mercedes had warned them about earlier and were now out of range of cell communication.

Kate walked to the bar and ordered a water. She wanted to have something in hand, but not something that made her tipsy. She needed to remain alert.

Beside her, perched precariously on her stool, sat Alexis's old Aunt Dottie. Kate wouldn't have been surprised if she hadn't left that spot since they'd pulled out of port. From the resigned look on poor Sal's face as he mixed the older lady yet another fuzzy navel, it appeared she was right.

"Why, just last week I finished another shawl. This one has tiny tea roses and silky white fringe along the edges." Dottie didn't seem to notice or care about the blank look on poor Sal's face. It seemed that knitting was her passion in her golden years, and she could talk for hours about every shawl and sweater and potholder she'd ever made. Just ask Sal. He was so dazed he didn't even bother to hide the fact he'd used one of the tools hidden inside the special prosthetic thumb Gideon had designed for him to open a can of fruit juice.

Kate bit back a laugh. That thumb of his had more attachments than a Swiss army knife, and she'd bet good money Sal found it a lot more useful than he ever had the real thumb he'd lost. Sal had been her parents' getaway driver on their heists and was always good at a quick escape. Too bad he couldn't pull one off now. Kate did her best to keep from laughing as Sal rolled his eyes and placed a fresh drink on the bar in front of Dottie, who hiccupped and then kept right on talking.

Kate turned away, refocusing her attention on the crowd of guests now looking at Ace, who was making his way toward her. So much for her time alone to think. He stood by her side as he made his announcement. "Attention please, everyone. Regarding the Wi-Fi service, rest assured we are working diligently to restore the service. Until then, won't you all join me and my beautiful wife on a tour of our lovely new yacht, The Leviathan?"

Ace offered Kate his arm, the picture of the doting, besotted husband. Her chest pinched again. If only that were true.

And if it was, what would you do? She didn't have an easy answer to that question as they started the tour in the luxuriously appointed salon with its modern contemporary furniture and lush Persian rugs. It was all done in tasteful shades of beige and cream and aqua. Very Mediterranean. The tour moved deeper inside the ship to a game room with multiple billiards tables, poker tables, a second bar, and a small private deck where guests could play shuffleboard. On the walls were more priceless artworks. Kate wasn't sure how much was forged and how much was real. The only thing she could say for certain was that Max had apparently gone all-out to bedeck the walls with the best images money could buy, reproductions or not.

Ned Parsons, of course, had his nose stuck right up against one again, studying it closely, his wire-rim glasses pushed close against his face. His wife Cindy was talking with Lawrence Martin, and apparently having a high time of it too, if their boisterous laughter was any indication. Kate made a mental note to find out more about the state of Ned Parsons's marriage when she had a chance.

Right now he was paying a bit too close attention to that copy of Monet's Water Lilies for her comfort. She'd checked the painting out earlier, with Gertie in tow, and it would take an expert to tell it was a fake. Was Ned an expert? Her intel on him only said he was from old money and his family collected art. He'd attended the functions at which artwork had been stolen. But lots of people had been at those.

Kate was about to head over and distract him when Ace took her arm and shook his head. "What?

Why? He seems a tad too interested in these paintings, wouldn't you say?"

"Hmm. Perhaps." He watched Ned for several seconds before shrugging. "Then again, all these people are very into art. That's why they're here, so maybe it's not that unusual. We don't want to scare them off before The Lemur makes a move."

"Maybe." Kate continued scanning the room, doing her best to ignore Sinclair Robinson, who kept giving her sly winks when he thought his wife wasn't looking. Icky. The man was old enough to be her father, first of all. The fact he'd tried to grope her in the storage closet still turned her stomach. And second … .

One of her false eyelashes took that opportunity to stick together, and Kate had to pry her eyelids apart. Unfortunately, she was still facing Sinclair's direction, and the whole incident gave the impression she was winking. At him. Ew She huffed and shuddered. "Darn it."

"What's wrong?" Ace frowned, running his hands over her arms, which only served to make her even more jittery. "You look fine. Did something happen? Tell me what's wrong."

"Nothing's wrong. Jeez." She shook off his touch and scowled. "My stupid eyelashes stuck together, and that yucky Sinclair Robinson keeps flirting with me after what happened in the storage closet earlier. Now he probably thinks I was winking at him and —."

Ace blinked at her several times before bursting out laughing. Her shock soon morphed into annoyance. "You do have the worst luck, don't you darling?"

"It's not funny. And stop calling me that," she hissed beneath her breath. "The last thing I want is for that disgusting man to think I'm interested in him like that at all. Ew."

"My little seductress." Ace grinned, then leaned in to nuzzle her ear in a false show of husbandly affection. "I know it's hard for any man to resist you, but for the duration of this trip, you belong to me." He ended his speech with a kiss on her heated cheek before tucking Kate into his side, his arm around her waist possessively as he shot Sinclair Robinson a hands-off stare.

Normally Kate would've pushed Ace away, but for some reason it didn't seem to bother her. In fact, she was glad for the warm, comforting support of his arm around her. Maybe Ace's glares would help keep Sinclair at bay.

The rest of the tour passed by in a blur — galley, staterooms, bridge, guest powder room. Before Kate realized it, they were back on deck and everyone was splintering off to eat or do their own thing. Several people mentioned going back to their rooms for naps after dinner, and a few of the ladies wanted to change and try out the shuffleboard deck.

While Ace went back topside to check in with Benny, Kate headed below deck to see how her father's progress was coming along with applying the dye to the storage room lock and the safe containing the painting.

She made her way down the main hallway past the guest cabins, then made a left into the narrow staff hallway. This hallway was where the storage room and maintenance office were located. It was quiet down here, with no one in sight.

Thud!

A loud kerfuffle sounded from the direction of the galley. Instincts on high alert, Kate jogged back the way she'd come and crossed over the main hallway again to head down the narrow right-side passageway instead. The noise grew louder, and several crashes and shouts echoed down the hall. Her pulse kicked up another notch.

Hidden in her costume was her weapon of choice — a small container of mace. Okay, most agents used guns and she had when she was in the FBI, but these days she felt better with mace. No matter what the weapon, no agent worth her salt would dare go out into the field unprepared, but she hated to pull her gun and blow her cover if she didn't have to.

Visions of her father, Vic, encountering The Lemur on his own filled her head. Had he attempted to apprehend the thief and a fight ensued? Or perhaps her mother had been surprised by the assailant while cooking dinner for their guests and fought back. Carlotta used to be an expert in karate, but she was older now. Were her skills still up to par?

Her parents were both well over retirement age. If she lost either of them without warning she'd be devastated. It was like running in a nightmare. She could see the galley doors ahead, but the faster she ran the farther away they seemed to get.

When Kate reached her destination at last, heart in her throat, she shouldered open the swinging doors prepared for the worst, and stopped short. Instead of the violence and gore she'd feared, Kate was confronted with a drunk Aunt Dottie throwing a fit in the middle of her mother's kitchen while Carlotta stood off to the side looking none too pleased. A plate of half-eaten dinner rolls sat on the island in the middle of the galley.

"What's going on?" Kate asked, out of breath from anticipation and adrenaline.

"What's going on is that all day I've been slaving away in here to prepare dinner for your esteemed guests tonight," Carlotta said, her usual hint of an Italian accent thicker now as she played the part of volatile master chef. "And what do I find? This woman sneaking in to eat half my freshly baked ciabatta. It's ruined. That whole display. Ruined! *Finito!*"

"Now you listen here, missy. I'm a paying guest in this establishment," Dottie said, her words slurred slightly, from alcohol or senility, Kate couldn't be sure. The older woman seemed distraught and disoriented, her movements jerky and her eyes unfocused. "No tip for you. *Comprende?* I want to speak with your manager."

Kate and her mother exchanged a worried glance.

"Dottie," Kate said, coming around the island slowly so as not to startle the older lady while cocking her head at her mother, indicating Carlotta should go find Vic and get him in here as soon as possible in case she needed reinforcements. Dottie was perhaps in her mid-eighties, but she still looked strong and had a good ten to fifteen pounds on Kate. If the elderly woman became combative, they could both end up getting hurt. Keeping her voice low and calm, Kate continued. "Dottie, sweetie, it's Connie Carlson. You're not in a restaurant, remember? You're on our yacht, The Leviathan. This is the kitchen, and it looks like you were enjoying some fresh ciabatta bread." She slipped an arm around Dottie's quaking shoulders as the woman continued to look around her, confused and disoriented. "Why don't you have a seat here on this stool and I'll get you a glass of water while we sort this out, okay?"

Dottie's scowl gradually faded into fear. She blinked several times, her eyes behind her glasses losing that dazed look and gaining clarity once more. "Where am I?"

"The galley." Kate grabbed a glass from the cupboard while keeping an eye on Dottie. "Do you remember how you got here?"

"No. I remember sitting upstairs at the bar talking to that nice man about my knitting, and then next thing I knew I was here with you. Oh, dear. I hope I didn't do anything too awful. I get these spells sometimes and everything just goes sort of black in my head."

Kate set the glass on the counter in front of Dottie, glad she'd sent her mother out of the room for her father. Kate had never really known her own grandparents, but spending time alone with Dottie made her imagine what they must've been like. Still, Alexis should really keep an eye on her aunt. The poor lady could've been injured or worse. "Do you know where your niece is?"

"Alexis?" Dottie sipped her water. "No. Last I saw her she was flirting with that sailor."

"Captain Benny, you mean?" Kate asked.

"Yes. He's rather large to be a sea captain, isn't he?"

The galley door swung open again, and Kate looked over expecting to see her parents. Instead, Alexis stood in the doorway, out of breath, her face flushed.

"Aunt Dottie." Alexis came into the galley then doubled over, putting her hands on her knees as she breathed deeply. "I've been looking all over for you. I thought maybe you'd gotten locked in a storage closet or something."

Relief washed through Kate. Alexis would take care of her aunt, and Kate could go about her business. She straightened and gave Dottie's shoulder one last pat before setting the plate of warm ciabatta in front of her again. "Eat a little more, Dottie. It will make you feel better. I just need to speak to your niece a moment."

Dottie patted her hand, then picked up a fresh roll and dug in.

Kate took Alexis by the arm and guided her back out into the hall, frowning. "You should keep a closer eye on your poor aunt. She could've easily gotten hurt in here if the cook hadn't been watching."

"I tried, but she's so fast," Alexis said, panting. "There one minute, then she's gone."

"Well, maybe if you flirted a little less with Benny you wouldn't be so distracted."

"What?" Alexis wrinkled her nose. "I wasn't with Benny. Okay, I was. But not at dinner. Aunt Dottie and I ate together, then she excused herself to use the restroom. I offered to go with her, but she wouldn't hear of it. So I waited. And waited. When I finally went to the powder room to see if she was all right, the door was locked and there was a sign saying it was closed for cleaning. I figured she'd maybe come down to our adjoining rooms instead. When I didn't find her, I immediately went searching. I've been at it at least half an hour."

Kate regarded her with a narrow gaze. She didn't seem to be lying, but The Lemur was known as a skilled pretender, able to slip in and out of guises easily. Maybe Dottie had just wandered off while Alexis was busy looking for the painting in the storage room. "Why did you think she'd be locked in a storage room?"

"What?" Alexis placed a hand over her still-heaving bosom.

"Seems like an odd place to bring up as a hiding place for your aunt." Kate tapped the toe of her sandal against the carpeted floor.

"Oh that." Alexis patted her bleached blond coif. "When we first boarded, my aunt mistook one of the storage rooms for our stateroom door and wandered in there by accident. I mean, the doors all look alike, so it was an honest mistake. Since then I've made it a point to tell her not to go in there again. That's the only reason I brought it up." Alexis stepped back and fiddled with her dress, checking her makeup in a mirror on the wall. "Now, if you'll excuse me, I need to collect my aunt and get back upstairs for dinner."

Chapter Five

K ate was just as uncomfortable that evening in her getup as she'd been before, although Ace had said she looked stunning, which she supposed meant something. Tonight she wore a black beaded evening gown with a formfitting skirt and flattering halter neckline. The rhinestone-encrusted stilettos, bracelet, and earrings from Gideon complimented the outfit to a T, even if the shoes were killing her feet. And she figured the removable heels on the shoes might come in handy if The Lemur finally decided to make a move and she had to give chase.

The yacht's salon had been transformed into a cozy restaurant, with the food served buffet style. Small, intimate tables topped in crisp white linen and flickering candles lined the room and spilled into the bar area. Tropical orchid centerpieces spiced the air with exotic scents. The muted sounds of jazz filtered from the sound system. Vic had suggested the arrangement, thinking it might get the guests to relax, and the dim lighting and mingling might encourage their thief to be braver and perhaps sneak downstairs to try to get into the storage room. Plus, with Sal serving up copious amounts of alcohol, tongues would hopefully soon loosen.

Ned made a beeline for Kate where she stood beside Ace near the start of the buffet table to greet their guests and direct them through the food line. Kate frowned at his outfit. Most of the guests were dressed in tuxedos, but Ned wore a brown suit, the cuffs of his shirt worn. Odd for someone from old money. Then again, people who were raised with that kind of money could get away with being eccentric.

"Mrs. Carlson, I wonder if I might inquire as to where you obtained your Monet's Water Lilies? I have it on good authority that the original of that particular is supposed to be hanging in the Met in New York right now. I'd hate to think that you and your husband were in any way involved in some heinous stolen art ring."

"That's rather presumptuous of you, Parsons," Ace said, glancing over at Ned, his expression as annoyed as Kate felt. "What exactly are you implying?"

Before Ned could answer, Alexis and her silicone boobs arrived.

"Oh, my. I'm so sorry I'm late," Alexis gushed. She stopped short of Kate and Ace, instead snaking her arm through Captain Benny's while he perused a tray of tiny lobster and crab puffs. "Getting Aunt Dottie ready after the episode in the galley this afternoon was challenging."

"Poor thing. I do hope she's okay," Kate said, eyeing the other woman suspiciously.

If she'd had trouble with her aunt, Alexis's expensive, immaculate designer gown and shoes didn't look any worse for the wear. She'd bet a million bucks those emeralds and diamonds around the gal's neck and wrists were real too, unlike Kate's rhinestone and glass baubles. Oh well. Kate would bet good money Alexis's fine jewels didn't pull double duty like her stuff did. She wouldn't trade her Gideon Crenshaw exclusives for anything.

She shot Alexis a censorious look as the woman all but draped herself over Benny, who appeared oblivious as he stuffed his face with food. "You should probably stay by her side this evening. Your aunt's back at the bar, and I doubt she should be drinking more at this point."

Kate tilted her chin toward where Dottie was sipping her favorite drink, though now Kate saw that Sal had put the Stoliano bottle back on the shelf as opposed to on the bar beside her. Probably a wise move. Dotty looked quaint even if her high-necked black satin dress and elbow-length gloves were a bit old-fashioned. In fact, Dottie looked as if she'd stepped off the set of a 1920s movie. Her gray hair was pulled back into a slick chignon at the base of her neck. The slightly glazed look from earlier in the kitchens had vanished. Tonight, Dottie looked every inch the regal queen.

Sal caught Kate's eye and gave her a little wink to let her know the drinks he served Dottie now were weak. Thank goodness. The last thing they needed tonight was Dottie invading her mother's kitchen again.

They presided over the buffet table until all the guests had filled their plates and congregated at various tables for the meal. Kate kept an eye out, noticing that Feisty excused herself to go to the bathroom, almost colliding with Dottie, and Ned disappeared after making his way to the end of the bar. Interesting.

Kate leaned over and whispered to Ace once they had filled their plates and sat at a table alone, "Does Sal have the glasses ready?"

"Yep. He's got them stowed below the bar. All we have to do is let him know we're ready and he'll fill them up." Ace looked around then smiled down at Kate. "And your father just gave me the signal the ink is spread. Now all we have to do is wait."

They dug into the food. Surf and turf, perfectly cooked. Kate made a mental note to compliment her mother, but she hardly enjoyed the food as she had one eye on the guests. It was getting hard to keep track now that they'd finished their first course and some had risen to get seconds while others beelined for the bar or restrooms.

When they'd finished eating, Vic, who was doubling as a bus boy, cleared their plates, and they stood, making their way toward the deck.

Feisty Robinson came up to Kate and Ace just as they neared the sliding glass doors. She had a tissue in hand and frown firmly in place. "I must say that the cabins on board this ship are terribly dusty. Sets my allergies off something fierce. You really should invest in some better housekeeping staff, my dear."

"Yes, my poor wife's been feeling quite under the weather today," Sinclair said, shooting Kate a lascivious glance. "Do tell me how you and your husband met, Connie."

"Oh, well. It's a very long boring story I'm sure you don't want to hear," Kate said, squeezing Ace's arm tighter to get his attention. "Isn't that right, honey?"

"What?" Ace looked perplexed for a moment before picking up on the topic of conversation. "Oh, yes. Well, same old story, chap. I saw my darling Snookums across the room and I just knew she was the one. I made it a point to talk to her that night and did my darnedest to sweep her off her feet." He raised Kate's hand to his lips and brushed them over the back of her hand, his gaze holding hers. She narrowed her eyes and looked away. "Still not sure what she sees in me, but I'll always be grateful for the chance she took on me."

"Oh, come now, Roger," Feisty said between sniffles. "I think we all know what she sees in you. Exactly how did you come by all your money again?"

Unfazed, Ace chuckled. "Why the old-fashioned way, Feisty. I inherited it. From the Tennessee Lottery."

They all shared a laugh at that.

"Really. That must have been quite an interesting turn of events. I'm guessing you didn't go to an Ivy League school then, old boy?" Sinclair asked, never taking his eyes off Kate. Even dressed in an expensive tuxedo, the man reminded her of a sleazy used-car salesman, all smarmy smiles and cheap lies. Kate barely managed not to gag. And Ace wasn't helping either, going totally off script and throwing out falsehoods to match Sinclair's whoppers.

"Sure did. Football scholarship. Until I got kicked out my senior year for a panty raid on one of the sororities." Kate hazarded a glance up at Ace and saw that while he was smiling, his eyes were cold enough to freeze water. He had always abhorred such sexist behavior and had fought against it whenever he encountered it at the FBI. It was one of the things Kate loved about him.

Had loved. Past tense.

Of course, the mention of panties got Sinclair's attention, and Kate was just glad she didn't have to talk to the creep anymore at the moment. Ace continued the small talk while Kate studied Feisty from under her enormous false lashes. She had to admit the woman did look sickly — all pale and frail, as if she'd jump at her own shadow—definitely not the right material for The Lemur. But then again, it could all be an elaborate ruse to throw them off the trail. Or a side effect of living with a creep like Sinclair. Talk about allergies. Ugh.

Kate tuned into the conversation again just as it ended. Both men chuckled hollowly and Kate sighed, the beginnings of a headache starting to pulse behind her eyes. She needed some quiet and fresh air, space away from Sinclair of the smarmy stares. "If you'll excuse us a moment, my husband promised me a moonlit walk on the deck. So nice to talk with you. Enjoy your cruise."

The words sounded fake, even to Kate's own ear. She all but tugged Ace outside to the deck and stopped at the railing, inhaling the fresh salt air. "God, that man is really insufferable, you know?"

"Yeah, I know." He dropped his southern accent. He moved closer and whispered, "But while we were eating and talking just now I was watching, and just about every guest in there slipped out at one point or another, and we haven't even finished dinner yet."

"I noticed." Kate took a sip of her sparkling apple juice and leaned her elbows back on the railing to watch as Dottie slowly made her way through the buffet line while the others chatted at their tables. Hopefully, at least one of these people had ink on their hands, meaning they'd visited the storage room downstairs.

Ace yawned. His arm brushed hers and she inched away. She hoped Ace wasn't trying to pick up where they'd left off. Though she had to admit that he was acting much nicer than she'd expected, she didn't want him to think it was anything more than business.

The last thing she wanted was for him to get any ideas that *he* was in charge. She'd been working for the museum longer than he had, so technically she should be the lead. Not only that, *she* was determined to be the one to catch The Lemur. She wanted to prove to Max, Ace and maybe even herself that she could do just as good a job as Ace on a mission. Maybe even more so, now that they were both working for Max.

Even though she knew she was fully competent, Kate had to admit she was worried that Max had hired Ace because he doubted her ability to solve things on her own. And yes, she'd frozen up in Stockholm during that incident with the snakes, but that was one time, and she'd gotten over that phobia. She'd proved that in Mexico. Besides, there weren't many chances for snakes to appear on this yacht. She didn't need Ace's help. All she needed was to prove that she could handle this on her own.

"What time is it?" Kate asked Ace.

He checked his watch. "Ten thirty. Why?"

She shrugged, then finished off her apple juice before setting her glass aside. "Listen, I know we said we wouldn't start using those cocktail glasses until everyone was done eating, but if all the guests have already slipped out, why not check now?" Kate craned her neck to look back into the dining area. "Everyone's here and it looks like they might pick at that buffet all night. It would be the perfect time. Plus, they only work for half an hour after contact with the alcohol, right?"

Ace exhaled and reached for Kate's hand again. "Actually, I was hoping to talk to you because we have a slight lull in things. Listen, I know that —."

Kate held up her hand to stop him. Was he going to apologize? Suggest a truce? Or even something more? Yeah. Definitely not ready for that conversation right now.

Summoning all her willpower, Kate pushed away from him and headed toward the bar, looking back at Ace over her shoulder. "I think it's the perfect time. I'm getting them from Sal now."

Kate's heart squeezed at Ace's resigned, hurt expression as he followed her. She felt bad for not hearing him out, but she couldn't deal with the shambles of their relationship and still keep her head in the game tonight. And right now, catching The Lemur was more important than anything else.

"Two whiskeys, on the rocks," she said to Sal, giving the signal they'd worked out. He nodded, pulling out Gideon's cocktail glasses and filling them with amber liquor before handing one to Kate and one to Ace. She gave him a little nod then clinked glasses with Ace and whispered, "Good luck."

They went their separate ways through the guests, mixing and mingling and always sipping, sipping, sipping to see if they spotted any incriminating dye on anyone's hands. By the end of it all, she'd wished she'd instructed Sal to fill the glasses with something other than whiskey because her head was getting a little fuzzy and she felt tipsy.

"There you are, my lovely," Sinclair said, coming up behind her. He slid his arm around her waist and propelled her toward the door that led down to the cabins below. Kate wanted to get away, but her mouth felt full of cotton and her legs didn't seem to want to work right. "Shall we meet again in our secret place, say five minutes?"

Inhibitions lifted, Kate wheeled around unsteadily, prepared to tell him exactly where he could shove his secret place. Thankfully Benny intervened in the nick of time. "Ah, Mrs. Carlson, I wondered if I might have a word with you about the navigational GPS software interface glitch from earlier."

She frowned at him, taking a moment to digest those words, which got all jumbled in her head. "Um, sure. Okay." She passed her glass off to Sinclair, who scrunched his nose and set it aside.

"The navigational what glitch?" she mumbled.

Benny hauled her back out on deck, and she gulped in fresh air. The cool breeze off the water helped clear her head a bit. After a few minutes, Kate snorted. "Thank you. Wow. That liquor really hit me hard."

"I could see that. And hey, I was winging it, okay?" Benny gave her an irritated stare. "Besides, it got rid of him, didn't it?"

"Yes." She rolled her eyes. "But he left before I got a chance to check his hands."

"How close do you have to be to see it?"

"A couple of feet, I'd say." Kate frowned as Benny took her elbow and guided her across the room to grab her glass again. "Where are we going?"

"Where do you think?" Benny cocked his head. "Look away. Just don't drink anymore. Pretend sip."

Kate did as Benny advised and raised the cocktail glass again, peering through the bottom at

Sinclair's fingers as he argued with Feisty. Her heart sped and her breath caught. Sure enough, ink glowed bright purple on his skin. She shifted slightly and checked out Alexis too, just to be safe, and… b*ingo*! More ink.

Both Sinclair and Alexis had been in the storage room this evening?

Together? Maybe.

She gave a small shudder at the thought, then grinned. Giddiness rose inside her. She couldn't wait to tell Ace that *she'd* found not one but two suspects. And yes, narrowing it down to one would've made it a lot easier for them, but still. She'd done it. She'd found two people with means, motive, and opportunity.

Take *that*, Ace Mason, agent extraordinaire.

And speak of the Devil, Kate glanced up and saw him walking back toward her through the dining room. She rushed to his side, eager to tell him what she'd found. Unfortunately, before she could, he dropped a bombshell of his own.

"I know who The Lemur is," he whispered, his warm breath stirring the hair near her temple as he leaned close. "Or at least I should say I've got it narrowed down to two people: Ned Parsons and Penny Martin."

"But that's not possible. I narrowed it down to Sinclair Robinson and Alexis Pennington."

Unless they're working together… she thought.

And life just became a whole lot more complicated.

Chapter Six
_____

"Four!" Kate said, flabbergasted. She tossed her rhinestone evening bag on the suite's coffee table and faced Ace. "Can you believe four of them had dye on their hands? Maybe we should start looking for the few people who *weren't* in the storage room tonight."

"Probably be easier that way." Ace snorted, then plopped down in one of the armchairs. "So, let's see. We've got Alexis, Sinclair, Ned, and Penny with ink stains, right?"

"Right." Kate smothered a giggle. All that drinking in pursuit of their suspect had left her a tad tipsy. She peered over at Ace sprawled in his chair, looking dashingly disheveled now, his bow tie undone and hanging loose from the open collar of his white shirt, the slight V revealing a hint of his tanned, toned skin beneath. Kate looked away fast, forcing her thoughts from Ace to the business at hand. "So, now what? The plan was to figure out the identity of The Lemur and notify Max that they'd stolen the fake painting and had it in their possession. Then he would board with the authorities and arrest them, right?"

"It was until we got a quadruple whammy." Ace rubbed his jaw, a hint of dark stubble shadowing his smooth skin. He looked more relaxed too, after several glasses of whiskey. She doubted it affected him as much, given their different sizes.

"Do you think all four of them could be in on it together?" Kate asked over her shoulder.

"You could be on to something there, kiddo," Vic said, strolling out of the guest bedroom. He walked over and gave Kate a kiss on the cheek before taking a seat opposite Ace. "The Golden Capers gang always worked together because it made sense. Split the duties, everyone works on the areas that cater to their strengths, and you also split the liabilities if one gets caught. With as many years as The Lemur's been practicing, it would make sense that there would be more than one person involved. As one ages out, another joins the team."

"That might explain why all the suspects weren't

at every event where paintings were stolen." Kate
had wondered about that in the dossiers she'd gotten
from Max. Then again, The Lemur didn't neces-
sarily have to be at an event to steal something. He
— or she — could have simply sneaked in the back
door. And not all the thefts took place during
an event.

Vic leaned back and seemed to contemplate that
for a moment. "But the MO has never changed in
any of the heists, so that speaks against a revolving
door of criminals. I don't know." He shrugged. "Plus,
I put dye on both the locks of the safe and the storage
room door, so maybe the others went in there for
another reason."

"Like what?" Gertie asked as she entered from the
suite's tiny kitchen. She was still dressed in her gray
maid uniform, a dish towel slung over one shoulder
and a bottle of Cuervo Gold in one hand. "I'd say the
only thing someone could get up to in there is no
good." She shrugged and looked at Kate. "You want
me to rummage around in their staterooms while I'm
'cleaning'?"

Kate chuckled as Gertie used air quotes for
emphasis. "Sure. Why not? But maybe do some
actual cleaning too, so you don't blow your cover."

Gertie gave a derisive snort and flopped into a

chair. She produced a shot glass from her apron pocket and unscrewed the cap of the tequila.

"You won't find the painting in anyone's room," Vic said. "It's still in the storage crate. I went down there right before you guys got back to double check."

"Well, that's good at least." Kate removed her high heels and sank down onto the sofa to rub her sore feet. The crystal shoes Gideon had designed for her were beautiful to look at but murder on a girl's instep. "Especially considering we don't have a clear suspect. I'd say our best next step is to eliminate each person with dye on his hands until we figure out which is The Lemur. And if it does turn out to be a group, then we chuck them all in the brig."

"The brig?" Ace chuckled. "Getting all nautical on me?" He winked, and she sighed. "It's a good plan, but we don't have that kind of time. Nor do we have an actual 'brig.' We dock in Venice at eight tomorrow night, and the reception starts immediately after that. If The Lemur is going to steal the painting and make a break for it, chances are high he or they will use the party as cover."

"We'd better get working then, huh?" She raised a sassy brow at Ace, then turned back to her father. "At least we know The Lemur will have to go back into the storage room to get the painting because it's still in the safe. With all the dye in there, they're bound to get more on them. Should make them easier to spot. I'll be sure to tell Sal to keep those glasses handy."

"But why were they all in the room in the first place?" Gertie asked.

"My guess is that some of them might have had another reason." Kate frowned, remembering how she'd run into Sinclair down there. He'd wanted to get his hands on something, but not the painting. "The real Lemur probably wanted to check out the painting and make note of its exact location for easy retrieval later, as we said before."

"So our thief may not even go back in until the party. But just in case, we should try to keep an eye on who goes in and out of that room," Ace said.

"That won't be easy with the narrow hallway. If we post someone to stand guard, that will scare The Lemur off," Kate said.

"Too bad that dang camera is busted." Gertie downed a shot and smacked her lips.

"I'm sure we can come up with something." Vic stood and stretched. "I best get back to the galley now. Carlotta was having a fit with one of the mixers not working correctly."

Kate frowned. "Really?"

He shook his head and smiled at Kate. "She was

never this much bother when she was making meals for us at home. I think my dear Carlotta's taken this role of chef a bit too seriously. Maybe she's bored with retirement." Vic headed for the door, then turned back. "As far as those ideas, why don't we all think about it tonight and meet again early in the morning? The whole gang. We can gather in the galley, where no guests will interrupt us as we brainstorm."

Chapter Seven

"That smells amazing," Kate said as she arrived in the galley the next morning to the sound of bacon sizzling and the sweet smell of maple syrup. The galley was scrubbed clean, the stainless steel almost blinding and the copper pots and pans that weren't being used for breakfast hanging from racks.

A quick glance around showed the whole Golden Capers gang was present and accounted for — Sal, Gertie, Benny, and of course her parents. Kate stopped by the stove to kiss her mom's cheek, then snuck a bite of cheese for the omelets before pouring herself a cup of strong black coffee and leaning against the counter beside Ace. She'd worn a cute red-and-white polka-dot jumper that clashed with her bouffant red wig, but Kate didn't care. And she and Ace kind of matched today, given his red shorts and white polo shirt. They looked like a couple, even if they didn't act like one except for show.

"All right, this strategy meeting is called to order," Kate said, gaining everyone's attention.

"Ugh. Bit early for strategy, eh?" Benny looked at her over the rim of his coffee mug.

"Hey, who's driving the ship?" Sal asked.

"Auto navigation," Benny slurped his coffee. "Plus I have one of the deck hands sitting watch. Captain can't be expected to watch over the yacht twenty-four, seven, you know." Benny patted his belly. "A man's got to eat."

"I just hope we don't have any more incidents with the ship lurching," Carlotta shot over her shoulder as she flipped pancakes. "Makes it hard to keep the kitchen running when everything is smashing about."

Benny cringed. "Sorry about that. I don't think it will happen again. I'll be sure to keep the ship upright until we reach port."

Other than the two incidents, it had actually been smooth sailing, much to Kate's surprise. She'd been skeptical about Benny handling the yacht. Sure, he had the appropriate license, but when it came to her parents' friends — and to Max — one never knew if the appropriate paperwork was real or something they'd procured by calling in a favor. But, given that they hadn't crashed into anything yet, it seemed Benny's skills were real, even if the paper might not be.

Benny took another slurp of coffee and then sighed, his captain's hat a bit crooked this morning as he scowled. "What are we strategizing about anyway? I thought things were going pretty well."

"We need to decide how we're going to catch The Lemur," Vic said, helping his wife by setting out dishes and flatware for everyone at the small teak banquette that sat along the wall. "Now that things have changed."

"Changed? I thought Max had all the T's crossed and the I's dotted before we set sail. And I've been hinting like crazy to all the guests that something rare and interesting is in the storage room." Sal frowned. "And what about those special glasses of Gideon's? Don't tell me I wasted all that good whiskey for nothing."

"It wasn't a waste," Kate said. "The glasses worked perfectly. Ace and I saw the ink clear as day.

We just ended up with more suspects than we'd anticipated."

"Yeah, four suspects," Gertie said. She tried to snag a piece of freshly fried bacon from the paper towel on the counter beside Carlotta, but got her hand slapped away for her efforts. "Where have you been anyway? We talked about that last night. I think you'd better start paying less attention to the guests and more attention to the case."

Bennie flushed but remained silent as Sal snickered at him.

"Seems like everyone dipped their fingers into that dye in the storage room," Ace said.

"Dang! Too bad that camera broke. We'd know exactly what each one of them was doing in there if we got it working," Vic said.

"Maybe it's better that it is broken." Gertie tried for the bacon again, this time snagging a small piece. "Some things can't be unseen, and with the way certain guests — and crew members — have been acting, there's no telling what kind of shenanigans people are getting up to in the storage room." She slid a sideways glance at Benny, who ignored her.

"Who had the ink on their hands?" Benny asked.

"Alexis, Sinclair, Ned, and Penny." Ace chugged a

glass of orange juice and then poured himself a second. Beside him on the counter were crumbs from the two doughnuts he'd scarfed down in the short time Kate had been standing there. Where the guy put all that food, Kate would never know. She had to watch every morsel she put in her mouth these days to fit into her formfitting evening gowns on this mission.

"Alexis, huh?" Benny halted mid-sip of his coffee. "She was upstairs earlier on the bridge. Asking me a lot of questions."

"Really?" Kate frowned. "Kind of early for her to be up, wasn't it?"

Benny shrugged a bulky shoulder. "She said she's an early riser."

"What kind of questions did she ask?" Vic set a plate of toast on the island counter.

"She wanted to know more about the layout of the ship. In between other things … ." Benny snagged a triangle of whole wheat toast to nibble on, keeping his gaze lowered. "But I didn't tell her anything she didn't already know, of course."

"Yeah," Sal piped in, his bushy black eyebrows knitted. "She was asking me some of the same stuff last night at the party. Asking me where this room and that was and where all the ladies' rooms were. If there was a public one down below. Said it was in case her aunt had another attack or something."

"Hmm." Carlotta turned from the stove with two plates full of omelets and pancakes in hand. She put one before Kate and the other before Ace before repeating the process until everyone had food in front of them. "Not sure I trust that one. A thief would need to know where things are located too. She could've been asking for her own purposes."

"I doubt she's The Lemur, though. Not exactly the calculating kind," Ace said generously, glancing at Benny before taking a bite of his eggs and cheese. As he chewed, he gave a happy sigh. "Carlotta, my sweet, you've outdone yourself again. This is delicious. Hard to imagine you're not a chef in real life."

"Most people don't know this, but that was once my dream," Carlotta said, before nudging Vic with her elbow. "Before I met this one and things took a different course. Everything works out in the end, though."

Kate sighed as her mother beamed at Ace, who was obviously trying to charm her. Ace used to flirt with Kate like that too. Not that she wanted him to do that now, but she knew he was doing it with her mother to get on her good side. Probably all part of his campaign to win Kate back. Kind of cute, in a way.

She shoved a large bite of omelet into her mouth. The eggs were light and fluffy and the cheese was salty and creamy — a perfect combination. Her suddenly grumpy outlook improved. Maybe Ace didn't have an ulterior motive for charming Carlotta. Maybe he was simply telling the truth. "He's right, Mom. This is spectacular. I never knew you wanted to be a chef."

"Thank you, dear," Carlotta said. "And yes. I loved to cook as a young girl. Then I had you and things changed. I was busy with work and taking care of you, and cooking didn't fit in. I regret nothing."

Carlotta's smile warmed Kate's heart. With a jewel thief for a mother and a con man for a father, Kate hadn't exactly grown up in a typical American family. Of course Kate hadn't known exactly what her parents did for a living when she was young. She knew it was something unconventional. Yet, they'd always taken the time to make sure everything else about Kate's childhood was normal and filled with love.

The gang finished their food amidst chatter about the day's activities and everyone's duties. Kate helped her mother and Gertie clear the dishes while the guys discussed the yacht's impressive bridge.

Kate had just finished drying her last plate when Ace moved in closer to her side and nudged her with his elbow, his warm grin disarming. "Say that again."

"Say what?" She gave him some serious side-eye.

"You know." He grinned. "That I'm right. I hear it so rarely from you that it bears repeating."

Heat prickled her cheeks. "I'm not saying it. But Mom's food was good."

"I'm glad you're eating. You're too skinny."

Kate raised a brow at him. "Since when are you looking?"

"I've never stopped looking," he said, his expression turning pensive. "You just stopped noticing."

Well, then. Kate glanced around at the rest of the group in the kitchen to find them all looking away fast, suddenly absorbed with interest in their food. *Great.*

Maybe she and Ace did need to talk about their relationship, but not in front of the gang. The Golden Capers Crew might be covert in their work, but personal secrets made the grapevine faster than the speediest Wi-Fi.

She finished her coffee and set her empty mug in the sink, doing her best to concentrate on the case.

"Well, I hate to say it, Benny, but until we know how Alexis got the dye on her hands last night she's still suspect. And it's possible she's trying to use her feminine wiles on you to glean information." Kate looked at Benny. "Although she seems to like you a lot. I noticed she's only flirting with you."

Benny nodded, swallowing a bite of bacon, and said under his breath, "She's done more than flirt."

"Ogling you is more like it," Sal teased. "She loves her some Bangkok Benny."

"Hey." Benny struck a pose. "There's a lot of me to love. What can I say?"

Snickers broke out through the kitchen, and some of Kate's tension lifted.

"Think you can use her flirting to find out more about her? About why she might have been in the storage room last night?" Ace asked him. "It would help to clear her a lot faster."

"Sure. Why not?" Benny finished his bacon. He frowned. "How about all those people with dye on their hands? Who's going to question them?"

"I guess Ace and I will. Wouldn't make sense for the staff to do it. Maybe Sal could get some good information at the bar. Unless anyone has a better idea." Kate turned to Vic. "Dad, did you come up with a plan?"

Vic pushed his empty plate away and folded his hands atop the table. "We need to figure out why each of them was in that storage room. Maybe mix and mingle with them upstairs during breakfast service. Gertie's going to make her housekeeping rounds, and will check their rooms for anything incriminating."

"And do some real cleaning too, right?" Kate winked at Gertie.

"Right." Gertie looked less than enthused by the idea but acquiesced. "Next time, though, I want a better cover. Not the cleaning lady, but a rich heiress or something where I can lounge around and look pretty all day."

Sal snorted. "That'd have to be a special assignment indeed. Hard to find twenty blind men who are all criminals."

Gertie tossed a wadded-up napkin at Sal's head, and more chuckles rang through the group. Then she pushed off her stool and stalked to the door, feather duster in hand, her nose in the air as regal as any queen. "I'm going to the storage room to get the vacuum."

"Yes, your majesty," Kate said, stifling a smile. "Guess the rest of us need to get to work too. Anyone have any questions? Remember. Meet and mingle.

We can meet back in our stateroom later today to report what we find out."

They all started toward the door except for Vic, who was staying to help Carlotta prep food for guests while Kate, Ace, Sal, and Benny all headed above decks to schmooze and snoop.

Chapter Eight

Ace stood at the end of the breakfast buffet, greeting their guests as they passed and keeping an eye on Kate. They'd gone in separate directions once they'd gotten topside, thinking they'd cover more ground working independently. It was a good plan, but it didn't stop him from thinking about – and worrying about—her. He cleared his throat against the knot of guilt that seemed to surface each time he thought of Kate these days.

He'd never meant to throw her under the bus, as she'd so eloquently described it, to the Bureau. If Ace had known she'd be fired he'd never have said anything. Or he would've lied. He'd never done that before in his career, lied under oath, but if it would've saved Kate's job and meant they'd still be together and happy he would've done it in a heartbeat.

Hell, it wasn't as if he hadn't already broken protocol by heading down to Mexico because his sources said Kate was in danger. He knew she'd needed his help, even if she never admitted it. She was stubborn that way, one of the many things he loved about her. And he'd almost died on that screwed-up mess of a mission, and would've done it a hundred times again just to have her look at him with the caring and affection as she had that day. To have her kiss him with such longing and gentleness. To have the chance to tell her he loved her … .

"Ah, Roger, darling," Alexis said, taking his arm and drawing Ace back to the present. She was wearing another diaphanous maxi-dress that billowed pastel tie-dyed colors in the breeze. "Such a lovely brunch, isn't it?"

"Yes. Fine." He noticed her gaze drifting to Benny again, who stood talking to Ned and Penny a few feet away. Ace made a mental note, then shifted his attention back to the task at hand—making Alexis think he was interested in her so he could try to figure out why she had the dye on her hands.

The brunch really was lovely. The long table was covered in gleaming stainless steel warming trays heaped with food. Turquoise accents added to the ocean atmosphere, and when it came to the food,

Carlotta had in fact outdone herself. There was every kind of breakfast treat you could imagine. Everything from croissants to kippers and tomatoes to turkey. And where in the world had they gotten a dolphin-shaped ice sculpture?

He shook his head and played the part of doting host to the hilt. "You look beautiful as always, my dear Alexis. Fresh as a daisy. Did you just come from your stateroom?"

"Yes." She glanced at Benny again, who was looking in their direction now, and gave him a slightly hurt look. "But a girl can't wait around down there forever, you know, for some man to come along." She shivered slightly and shook off the frown puckering her brow.

"I can't imagine you have to wait around much for men." Ace tried to keep a straight face as he charmed her.

Alexis smiled and turned her attention to him. "Now aren't you nice. Your wife is very lucky." Her attention wavered, and she looked around. "Say, have you seen my aunt Dottie? She took off while I was in the shower and I haven't seen her since. The poor thing's been wandering around a bit more confused than normal lately. Why, I even had to search for her again last night down there. I tried all the doors, but most were locked. I finally found her trying to enter the Parsons' stateroom. Good thing they weren't there at the time. I got her in hand and escorted her back to bed, then promptly locked the door from the outside. That way she'd have to go through my adjoining room if she wanted to get out."

"Don't be too hard on her. It can be confusing down there. I think some of the other guests have been getting lost too," Ace said. He was fishing to see if Alexis would mention seeing any of the other guests near the storeroom.

Alexis frowned. "You don't say? Thankfully no one has tried to get into my room. Though I did hear that Feisty Robinson making a ruckus outside in the hall. I was half afraid she was going to come in. But she moved along." She leaned close to Ace and lowered her voice. "Probably caught that no-good husband at something in the storage room down the hall from me."

Ace raised a brow. "Hmm. Maybe. The storage room seems to be popular, but there's really no reason to go in there."

Alexis gave him a sharp—and if Ace wasn't mistaken—somewhat guilty look. "Right. Of course there isn't." She stood on tiptoes, glancing around. "Now where did Aunt Dottie go? Looks like I need to go searching again. I need to keep her close today, lots to do getting her dolled up for the reception. Excuse me."

Ace patted her hand as she pulled away from him, the cloying smell of her heavy perfume making him sneeze. Funny thing, when he mentioned the store-room Alexis didn't say that one couldn't get in there because it was locked. Was that because she'd never tried to get in or did she have the lock-picking skills of The Lemur?

He pondered what Alexis had just told him. Looking for Dottie was a great excuse to be down by the storage room, and if she was trying all the doors that would explain the ink on her hand. But was it a true story or had she just told him that so she'd have an excuse as to why she'd been down there?

He was about to go tell Kate his findings when he was waylaid by Penny. He plastered on a fake smile and bowed his head slightly. "Ah, good morning, Penny. How did you sleep last night?"

"Very well, thank you," she said, stepping closer to Ace. Where Alexis had looked like an exotic bird of paradise with her frothy colors, Penny Martin looked like a prison warden, all cool grays and sensible sneakers. "Exactly how many staterooms are there aboard this ship?"

"Oh, the standard amount," Ace answered vaguely, wondering why she was asking. It couldn't be because she wanted to try to figure out which door was the storage room. She had ink on her hands, so she'd already been in there. "Did you have any trouble finding your way to your stateroom last night? Perhaps mistakenly wander into another room by accident? I heard poor Dottie did that."

Penny laughed, a shrill, unpleasant sound. "Don't be absurd. I have a great sense of direction. Though it is easy to get turned around below decks, so I can see why poor Dottie would get confused. I think I have a pretty good handle on the ship's layout. Now, about those staterooms, are they all occupied this voyage?"

"Two are empty," Ace said. "We invited only the most interesting people in the art world. I had no idea you were so familiar with ships."

Penny frowned. "Well, of course my family had a yacht. How many exits are on board here?"

Was she planning an escape? "The usual amount. Why do you ask?"

"Just wondering. I mean all this lovely artwork that you've collected and I wondered how you got it in and out. Where did you say you bought your art?"

"All over." Ace tried to steer the conversation back

to the storage room. "I imagine you've seen all the pieces we have hanging, even in the lower corridor."

"Most of them. I assume you bought some from galleries?"

Ace was becoming exasperated. His questioning was going nowhere and he was growing tired of her countering his every question with one of her own, as if he was being interrogated. It was the slight nasal tone of her voice that did it, he decided. Between Penny's whine and Alexis's deadly scent, the two women had him well on the way to a migraine.

He finally took a break in Penny's questioning and excused himself to wander to the railing for some fresh air, his mind still ticking through what he'd learned.

He wasn't sure about Alexis's story about searching for her aunt below decks. Frankly, Alexis didn't strike him as intelligent enough to be The Lemur, but he knew from experience that many criminals acted not very bright as a smokescreen.

Penny, though, was another matter entirely. She seemed plenty shrewd enough, and she'd even blatantly denied being lost. In fact, she'd claimed she had a great sense of direction and knew the layout of The Leviathan, so how did she get dye on her hands? If she really did know the layout she must have gone in the storage room on purpose. And if she was in there, that meant she picked the lock. Could she be The Lemur? If so, then why would she admit to knowing where all the rooms were? It would be smarter to play dumb, like Alexis.

Ace shook his head and started toward his stateroom. So far his mission to get information out of the suspects had left him with more questions than answers.

———

KATE STOOD across the deck from Ace, again trying her best to dodge Sinclair Robinson and his skin-crawl-inducing, lascivious glances. So far she'd managed to avoid him by squeezing behind a table and keeping the rest of the guests between them as she navigated around the deck. She was hoping Benny or Ace would've gotten stuck with the guy, but no such luck.

"You really do look spectacular today, Connie my love." Drat! Sinclair had found her. He stopped a few feet away to give her a head-to-toe appraisal that made Kate want to take a bleach bath. At least her shoes were more comfortable today — a pair of cute raffia wedges that soothed her aching toes from the night before. Now if she could just get rid of this creep she'd be all set. And yes, he'd had ink on his hands too, but she shuddered to think where else those hands might have been.

Sinclair stepped in beside her again, leaning in far too close for Kate's comfort. "Perhaps you and I could make another quick sojourn to the supply closet later, eh?"

His breath stank of grease and garlic from his breakfast, but Kate avoided scrunching her nose through sheer force of will. "I don't think that would be a good idea."

She did her best to sidle away and put some space between them, but he stuck to her side like a barnacle. His blue polo shirt and plaid Bermuda shorts only served to highlight his pallid skin and lack of muscle tone.

Sinclair's mention of the storage room put Kate on high alert. How many women on the ship did he go down there with? Was the ink on Penny's and Alexis's hands caused by a trip to the storage room with Sinclair? And because the room was locked, how in the world was he getting in? Maybe a tryst wasn't the only reason he went into that room.

"You seem distracted, darling Connie," Sinclair said, trying to take her hand before she pulled away.

His smile was a bit too wide and his tone a bit too eager. He followed her line of sight across the deck to Ace. "Marital woes?"

"Not at all." She forced a smile, answering a tad too quickly. "I do wonder, though, how did you get into that storage room? The staff is supposed to keep it locked and ... well, you know how hard it is to get good help. I want to make sure they are doing their jobs."

"Locked? Yes, right. Well, it wasn't locked, as you know, because you must have unlocked it."

"You mean when you found me in there?" Much as Kate didn't want to be reminded of that little interlude, it was necessary to get more information from him.

"Found you? Well if you want to put it that way ... I mean, you did slip me the note requesting my presence."

"Note?" What was he talking about? This was the first she'd heard of any note. But now that she thought about it, he had implied that she was waiting for him in that room. Had someone else slipped him a note, or was he making this whole note business up in order to have an excuse for being in the room?

Sinclair stepped closer and lowered his voice. "Now, Connie, if you want to play coy about the note

I understand, but I will have you know that you are the only one that I want to go into the storage room with. I swear."

Kate studied him. She doubted that was true, and she knew he was lying at least about being in the room. He had the ink on his hands, and that was only applied after he'd accosted her in there. Did he have a different reason for being in there? Was his octopus act upon finding Kate there merely a cover-up?

Sinclair moved even closer, causing Kate to stand back. "I sincerely do hope your husband is keeping you happy. You seem a little distracted this morning. You might need some relaxation before the reception tonight ... I am so looking forward to that."

Kate fought to keep from making a disgusted face. "I'm fine and *very* happy with my husband. This trip is so exciting for a country gal like me. I'm just a little tired, I suppose."

"Well, I slept like a baby last night," Ned said, joining them. Kate had never thought she'd say it, but she'd never been so glad to see stuck-up, irritating Ned Parsons. She straightened and moved away from Sinclair again. This time, thankfully, the letch stayed rooted to the deck.

"So, Ned," Kate said, turning her attention to the

new arrival. "Have you had a chance to explore the yacht? I hope you didn't get lost below deck?"

Ned gave her a peculiar look. "I haven't done much down below. I've been too busy inspecting all your artwork up here. Such fine pieces."

"We have some hanging in the hallway below too." Kate kept her tone light as she dangled a carrot before him. He'd had ink on his hands, and possible a secret identity to boot. "Have you seen those? I thought someone mentioned you being down there."

The color drained slightly from Ned's thin face, and his tone turned sharp. "No. I haven't. Well aside from the one near my stateroom, of course. I've seen that one, but I haven't been exploring below deck. That would simply be inappropriate to be sneaking around down there."

"Oh, well those paintings are just as pretty." Kate took in his blanched appearance and nervous tremble. Nerves or guilt? Given what Max had in the dossier on Ned and his endless search for his family's antiquities lost during World War II, it was much more likely he was here to see if any of the lost bounty was on board the yacht and lay provenance to it, rather than steal it out from under their noses. Still, she couldn't rule him out completely, and he was acting strangely now that she'd mentioned him snooping downstairs.

Ned fiddled with his tie nervously as he inched away. "Excuse me. I must find Cindy. We're going to get some sun before we nap and get ready for the big reception tonight."

Kate wasn't about to be left alone with Sinclair, so she inched away too. "Good idea. I must find my husband as well."

Kate took off across the deck without waiting for a reply.

Ace smiled warmly as Kate joined him at the rail. The fresh sea air smelled of salt and helped drive Sinclair's groping from her mind. She inhaled deeply and glanced sideways at her partner. "Everyone seems excited about tonight's reception."

"Yep. Had a couple of them ask me about docking time. And a couple more still complaining about the lack of cell service."

Kate chuckled. "Yes, most people can't disconnect. But one of these folks is The Lemur. He might have another reason to want cell service, especially if he is trying to contact an accomplice at the dock."

"Exactly my thought."

"I saw you talking to Alexis and Penny. Were you able to find out anything more from either of them?"

Ace told her about what he'd heard from both women, then shook his head. "I doubt it's Alexis. That aunt of hers keeps her so busy searching for her that she hasn't time to steal anything."

As if on cue, Dottie tottered by, scowling and cursing at a huge smartphone in her hand. Today, she wore a bright-yellow jumpsuit that made her resemble a ripe banana. Kate bit back a grin and stepped forward to put her arm around the older woman's shoulder. She caught Ace's eye over the top of Dottie's head. "Good morning, Dottie. Don't you look bright and cheerful this morning. Is there anything I can help you with?"

"No. I'm trying to send a text with this stupid thing and I can't seem to get it to work." Dottie shook the phone so hard Kate feared she'd hurl it into the sea.

"Ah, let me see." Kate pried the device from Dottie's fingers, noticing the woman's red nail polish was smeared and chipped. Her skin looked red and puffy, as if she'd scrubbed it raw. Kate frowned, her tone concerned. "Dottie, what happened to your hands?"

"Oh." The older lady immediately hid them in the pockets of her jumpsuit. "That's why I wore gloves last night. My nail polish looks awful, doesn't it? Too bad I won't be able to get a fresh manicure until we dock in Venice. I'm too old to paint them myself anymore. Too unsteady, and it gets everywhere. Alexis tries to do them for me when she can, but she's been so busy on this cruise."

Kate felt sorry for the poor thing and pulled Dottie close again. "Well, I'm sorry to say that if you were trying to text the mainland to get an appointment it won't work. Captain Benny's been trying to fix the problem, but as of this morning we're still without cell service. Maybe you could spend the next few hours relaxing in the sun? Take a break from technology. That's what I plan to do until we reach Venice."

"Yes, I suppose so." Dottie took her phone back from Kate and shoved it in her pocket. "First, though, I should go back downstairs and get my gloves. Lord knows I don't need these hands looking any worse than they already do. Thank you, my dear."

Kate and Ace exchanged a look as the older lady tottered off again.

Chapter Nine

"So, of the two suspects I've talked to, I've got a front-runner," Kate said while she and Ace waited for the rest of the gang to arrive in their suite for another briefing.

The afternoon lull saw most of the passengers either dozing in the sun or napping in their cabins. Kate had taken off her wig and tossed it on the coffee table, and removed her shoes. It felt good to sit and relax for a moment instead of playing her part.

"Really? Who?" Ace sat beside her, genuinely interested in her assessment.

"Ned. He acted awfully strange at breakfast when I asked him about being below decks. I would have said Sinclair, but he's so busy trying to cop a feel that he wouldn't have time to steal a painting."

"Or that's what he wants you to think," Ace said.

"Not sure he's that cunning. I have a different front-runner as my prime suspect."

"Really? Who?" Kate asked, hating the catch in her voice as Ace stretched his arm along the back of the sofa behind her head.

"Penny Martin."

"Penny?" Kate frowned. "She seems a bit dull to be The Lemur. Very prim and proper."

"Yeah." He toed off his shoes, rested his feet on the glass coffee table. "Perfect disguise. And I get this weird feeling when I talk to her. Feels like I'm the one under investigation or something."

"Yeah, she is a weird one." Ace's hand brushed her shoulder, and Kate suddenly became hyper-aware of him. The room seemed small, cozy, and sitting here on the couch beside Ace and talking about the case seemed ... right.

"What about Sinclair? Has he been bothering you?" Ace asked.

Kate's heart leapt at the look of concern on Ace's face. She'd forgotten how good it felt to have someone care about her that way. "Nah, he's harmless. Well, maybe not harmless, but he hasn't bothered me much. He did say something odd, though."

"What's that?"

"He was under the impression that I'd passed him

a note that first day asking to meet him in the storage closet."

Ace snorted. "Seriously?"

"Yep."

"Well, he must be lying. Unless you're up to something I don't know about."

"Hardly." While they'd been talking, Ace's thumb had been rubbing her shoulder. It was distracting. But for some reason, this time, Kate didn't want to move away. She'd forgotten how much she missed bouncing ideas off of him and the close connection they used to have.

"So who do you think is the most suspicious?" Ace's voice was rough. Kate glanced up at him. When had she slid so close to him? His lips were barely a foot away. Something flickered in the depths of his gray eyes.

"Well, I ..." She could barely squeak the words out, her heart was hammering so fast.

Ace leaned down toward her. It seemed the most natural thing in the world to tip her mouth up toward him and close her eyes.

Before their lips met, however, the door to the suite burst open, and Gertie walked in. They jumped apart as Gertie plopped down in the armchair across from them, seemingly oblivious to their near-kiss and waving a paper in her hand. "Guess what I found in Sinclair Robinson's room. A naughty little note."

Kate took the note: "'Meet me below deck in the storage room.' So there really was a note."

Gertie's face fell in disappointment. "You already knew about the note?"

"Sinclair mentioned it. Thought I sent it," Kate said.

"Did you?" Gertie smirked.

"No!"

"What's that on the corner? Blood? I bet he didn't mention that." Gertie pointed to a small smudge that darkened one corner of the otherwise pristine white paper. The color vaguely reminded Kate of Dottie's nail polish, but that wouldn't make sense. Why would dear old Aunt Dottie slip smarmy Sinclair a note? She certainly wouldn't want to meet him for hanky-panky.

"I don't think it's blood." Kate held the note up to the light. "Thankfully no one has died on this cruise. I think it might be nail polish. It looks like the color Dottie wears."

"You think the old lady and Sinclair have some-thing going on?" Ace joked.

"Just because people age doesn't mean the good times are over," Gertie said, shrugging. "Maybe she wanted a little nookie in the supply closet. A little bark in the dark. A —."

"Please! Ew." Kate held up a hand and couldn't stop from wrinkling her nose in disgust. "Though I wouldn't put it past Sinclair."

Gertie nodded. "Yeah. He's such a creep. And he's no looker, so maybe he realized he can't be that selective. Wife seems nice, though."

"Or maybe the note is from Alexis," Kate suggested.

"Alexis? Nah. She only has eyes for Benny this trip. Lots of people have nail polish," Ace said.

"Hard to believe, but apparently Sinclair has an admirer somewhere." Kate handed Ace the note. "And unfortunately, this only supports my theory that we can take him off the suspect list. He went to the storage room hoping for a romantic rendezvous, not to steal the painting."

"But that was before we put the dye on the lock," Ace pointed out.

"True, but he might have gone back later. Our first rendezvous was interrupted."

"Hmm. Maybe." Ace sat back, his bunched shoulders relaxing slightly. "Okay. But if he keeps bothering you, tell me and I'll take care of him. Permanently." He looked away, tossing the note back on the table and scrubbing a hand over his face. "I think we can safely take Alexis off that list too. She was downstairs looking for Dottie half the night. Said she found her aunt trying to get into the wrong stateroom."

"Oh, poor Dottie." Kate slumped back against the cushions. "I've seen how confused she gets. I've found her wandering around a few times. I agree. Alexis has her hands full babysitting her aunt. No time to steal anything. We have limited time, so let's not focus on her."

Vic and Carlotta walked in, followed by Benny and Sal.

Kate and Ace explained what they'd found and why they believed moving Sinclair and Alexis to the bottom of the suspect list was correct.

"Sounds reasonable," Benny said. "My Alexis would never do anything so dastardly."

"Your Alexis?" Gertie asked, dark brow raised. "Since when?"

Benny colored about twelve shades of puce. "Oh, well. I didn't mean it like that."

"Really?" Carlotta sat forward. "How did you mean it?"

"Stop giving him a hard time, dear." Vic pulled

his wife back to his side. "Can't you see our Benny's in love?"

"Am not!" Benny looked away fast. "Okay, maybe a serious like, but not love."

"Aw, that's sweet." Kate patted his hand. "Just don't fall too hard too soon. Not until we've got The Lemur behind bars. Just because we're moving her to the bottom of the list doesn't mean she's in the clear."

"I won't." Benny frowned. "I'm not as innocent as all of you seem to think."

"All right, gang. So, we're focusing on Ned and Penny as our best bets for The Lemur," Kate said, standing to pace the room. She needed to burn off some excess energy. "We've got a couple of hours until we dock. Let's keep an extra-close eye on all of our guests, suspects or not. If anyone sees anything out of the ordinary, let Ace or I know immediately. We can't risk The Lemur getting away now. Not when we're so close to catching him after all these years." Kate could almost taste the victory of an arrest. No way would she allow the thief to escape now, no way would she let anyone else take credit for solving the case. She needed this one. Badly.

"Right. Everyone rest up for the reception tonight. The Lemur's bound to make a move, and we have to be ready."

Chapter Ten

An hour or so later, Kate was on deck in a chaise lounge, a frou-frou drink by her side as she watched Ned and Penny from behind her sunglasses. A steady, warm breeze blew from the sea, keeping her from getting too hot and carrying with it the scent of salt and seaweed, and the caw of gulls swooping low to nab the morsels of bread Ace tossed their way.

Ace. Kate sighed. She still hadn't figured out what she was going to do about him, other than the fact she didn't want him discovering the identity of The Lemur before she did. She might still be half in love with him — or more than half, truth be told — but that didn't dampen her competitive streak. And boy, he did look fine in those board shorts, she noted not for the first time, as he bent over to grab a slice of bread he'd dropped.

The slight tingle on her skin said it was time to reapply her sunscreen, so Kate pushed to her feet and headed indoors, only to find Penny right by her side again. It was funny, really. Kate was beginning to wonder if she was keeping an eye on Penny or Penny was keeping an eye on *her*. She kept turning up each time Kate went inside to use the restroom or get a fresh drink. And wasn't that just the same thing Ace had mentioned?

Still, Kate couldn't pass up an opportunity to chat up one of their top suspects. She smiled blandly at Penny. "Fancy meeting you here again."

"That sun is killer," Penny said, at least having the decency to look a bit ashamed. She was dressed in the saddest brown swimsuit Kate had ever seen. It resembled those old-fashioned swimming costumes women wore in the twenties, covering more skin than it revealed. "I'd hate to end up wrinkled like a raisin because of it."

"Yes, that would be awful." Kate seriously doubted enough sunlight could penetrate that thick Lycra to tan Penny's skin, let alone cause any damage to her pasty complexion. Kate pulled out her tube of sunscreen, continuing to make idle chit-chat as she rubbed lotion into her freckled skin — the bane of natural redheads everywhere. Thankfully, her own natural copper color wasn't anywhere near the fire-engine-red monstrosity on her head. A flash of movement caught Kate's eye in the dim inner cabin, and she glanced over to see Dottie wandering around, looking lost. "Oh, dear. Poor old thing. Looks like she's confused again."

"Yes." Penny frowned as she followed Kate's gaze. "I suppose we should help her."

"Yes, we should." With Penny's help, Kate got Dottie back out on deck and seated at a table under an umbrella. "Dottie, honey. Do you know where you are?"

"What?" Dottie blinked blankly up at Kate. "What's going on?"

Sal came over with her favorite drink, and some clarity finally returned to Dottie's expression. "Ah, that's better," Dottie said after draining half the glass. "Blasted hot out here, isn't it? Is it time for the reception yet?"

"No, Dottie." Kate exchanged a worried look with Penny. "That's not for a few hours yet."

"Oh, right. Of course." Dottie sipped more of her drink. "I knew that."

"Oh, thank goodness!" Alexis rushed to the table

where they stood, looking frazzled. "I've been searching all over for her. I was afraid something horrible might have happened. Where did you find my aunt?"

"She was wandering around inside," Kate said, studying Alexis's flushed face and fluttering hands. She seemed genuinely upset about her aunt's disappearance, despite her slightly disheveled appearance — with that wrinkled caftan and messy hair, Alexis looked as if she'd rolled right out of bed. A spot of red on her collar caught Kate's eyes. A smudge of what appeared to be nail polish — the same shade Dottie was wearing. Memories of her conversation from earlier with the older woman resurfaced. She'd mentioned being too unsteady to do her own nails, that she needed help. She also mentioned Alexis filled in for Dottie's regular manicurist sometimes. But a glance at Dottie's nails showed they were in the same sad state as before. And Alexis's nails were done in a French manicure. No color at all. So where had that splotch of red come from?

Before Kate could ask, Penny cursed under her breath and turned away, blinking her big brown eyes rapidly.

"What's wrong?" Kate asked, concerned.

"I think I got some of that sunscreen in my eyes," Penny said, covering her face.

"C'mon." Kate led her back inside and grabbed a box of tissues. As Penny dabbed her watering eyes, Kate took the opportunity to discover more about their new top suspect. Max had sent them full dossiers on all their passengers aboard the yacht, but Kate wanted to find out what wasn't on paper. "Where are you from, Penny? Originally?"

"What?" Penny seemed a bit startled by the question but quickly recovered. She stared in a mirror, doing her best to salvage her makeup. She met Kate's eyes in the reflection. "A little town in the Midwest. Middle of nowhere, really. I'm sure you've never heard of it. No one has."

"Try me," Kate said, forcing a polite smile. "I'm from the Midwest and was quite good at geography in school."

"Really? I was awful at it. I preferred art and music and dancing. How about you?"

Kate didn't miss the way she deftly changed subjects. Just as Ace had said she'd done with him. Penny was definitely evasive, but she was done with her makeup and there was no way to keep her inside without appearing suspicious, so Kate followed her back out on deck and resumed her seat in the chaise lounge. She'd wondered if The Lemur would try to steal the painting this afternoon, but everyone was exactly as she'd left them, no one missing. So much for *that* theory.

Chapter Eleven

That evening Kate was in her suite getting ready for the reception. If The Lemur was going to make a move, tonight was the optimal time. Ace wasn't around, which was odd, but she tried not to let it get to her. After all, they weren't a couple anymore, even though they were playing one for this mission. For all she knew he could be off somewhere flirting with Penny, no matter how unlikely that seemed. Penny wasn't exactly his type and she was married, even if that union smacked of convenience. Unexpected jealousy pricked Kate's chest before she tamped it down. And darn Ace and his chivalrous nature. He seemed genuinely concerned about Alexis too.

For this evening she'd chosen a different rhinestone dress, this one with an ombre fall of shimmering stones that began clear and ended up black near the floor-length hem. It really was a sight to behold, gorgeous, even if Kate was the only one looking at the moment. She'd worn the crystal shoes and jewelry Gideon had made for her as well. Carlotta had even managed to find time to style Kate's wig while she'd been in the shower, sweeping all that red hair up into a dramatic twist and placing several rhinestone clips amongst the curls. She looked good. Better than good. She looked amazing, if Kate said so herself.

As she stared at her reflection she made a final run-through of all aspects of her disguise to make sure she hadn't forgotten anything. Wig? Check. Colored contacts? Check. Extra padding in her bra and fake eyelashes out to there? Check and check. She looked nothing like herself, which was too bad because her ever-mysterious boss, Maximillian Forbes, was supposed to make an appearance at tonight's reception once they docked.

Thoughts of actually seeing Max in person perked Kate up. Thus far her attempts had always been foiled by Max's assistant, Mercedes. Well, tonight, she intended to change that. Ace was supposed to present a painting to Max as a gift for the museum. That very painting, a lovely Monet, had actually been in storage at the museum for decades. Max had circulated a story that Connie and Roger had purchased it from an old, established family and was donating it to the museum — another act to solidify their standing as patrons of the arts.

Finished, Kate walked out into the living room just as Ace finally decided to show up. He glanced at her as he closed the door behind him. "You look gorgeous."

His tone and the expression on his face were genuine, and Kate's heart flipped. "Thanks."

They stood there staring at each other for a few long seconds before she finally squeaked out, "Where were you?"

Ace walked into the bedroom to get ready, talking through the open doorway as he went. "To the storage room to check on the painting. I didn't want any last-minute surprises." He stripped off his polo shirt, and Kate did her best not to ogle his tanned skin and ropes of muscles. "I ran into Gertie. She was getting her vacuum out of that small closet down there right across the hall. She saw me open the door and came in to look over my shoulder. She's awfully protective of that forgery. Says it's one of her best. Maybe we should give it to her after this is all over, eh?"

"We could, I suppose," Kate said, making a pretense of fiddling with her shoes. Anything to stop herself from staring at half-dressed Ace. "She's earned it."

"Yep. She has." Ace headed for the bathroom. "I'm going to take a quick shower. Be right out."

Once the door closed behind him and the sounds of running water filled the room, Kate wandered out onto the balcony to watch the sunset. After all the work they'd put into this mission, what if The Lemur didn't strike at all? Maybe being in such close quarters made the thief feel too exposed, that stealing the painting would be too risky. It bothered her that after an entire day they'd still not narrowed it down to a single suspect.

She shook off those thoughts as she squinted at the horizon, now colored with brilliant streaks of gold and purple and pink. A faint coastline darkened the horizon. Venice. At last. She shook her head and stared down at the darkening waters of the Adriatic. No, most likely The Lemur would wait until the reception was in full swing and the yacht was filled with partygoers to make his move. Just as Max had predicted.

Behind Kate, the bathroom door opened again and the sound of heavy footsteps padding across the carpet echoed back into the bedroom. She hazarded a glance over her shoulder at Ace, freshly shaven and hair damp, a white towel slung low around his hips. She bit her lip and looked away fast. Chemistry had never been a problem for them. It was everything else between those times that was the hard part.

A few minutes later the red-orange sun had slipped beneath the black surface of the water and Ace had finished dressing. Kate wandered back into their suite to find him adjusting his bow tie in the mirror. He caught her eye and grinned, sending her knees wobbling again. He really did clean up well.

"How do I look?" he asked, doing a slow turn in front of her. "Does Roger Conway pass inspection?"

"Yes," she said, her tone going a bit breathy. The way his broad shoulders filled out his black tuxedo and the cut of the suit accentuated the long trim lines of his body, there wouldn't be a woman on the cruise who could take her eyes off him. Kate certainly couldn't. "Connie Conway approves."

Ace chuckled and turned away again, clearing his throat and thankfully steering their conversation back to safer territory. "I told Vic to keep an inconspicuous eye on anyone who might wander below decks tonight. We don't want to be too obvious and scare off The Lemur when he finally decides to make his move. Vic has an excuse to be down there as part of the maintenance crew."

"Good idea," Kate said, forcing herself to look anywhere but at him and fumbling her way back to the sofa. "Oh! We should give him one of the rings Gideon made so he can signal us if he sees anyone."

"Already thought of that, and he has it." Ace grinned and joined her on the sofa, sitting a bit closer than necessary. "See? Great minds think alike. Have to say that ring is pretty amazing. Great stealthy way to communicate in tight quarters without anyone noticing."

It sure was, and Kate needed to be on the receiving end of it. If Vic spotted someone taking the painting, this was her chance to bring the thief down. Kate glanced at Ace's hands, then craned her neck to look on the sink in the bathroom where she'd put it the night before. It wasn't there. "Where's the other ring?"

"In my pocket." He patted his left pec and then stretched an arm out across the back of the sofa again, his warmth surrounding her. "It's kind of small, but I'm going to put it on my pinkie when we go out to the reception."

Kate held out her hand. "It fits me pretty good."

Ace shook his head. "No way. Too dangerous. I

think it's best if I receive the signal. Then we can both go down and capture The Lemur together."

Kate's narrowed eyes darted from Ace's face to his pocket. Was he trying to cut her out or did he really want to capture The Lemur *together*? It was selfish, but Kate wanted all the credit. If they had to be partners in the future — as Max had implied when he'd hired Ace — she'd do things together *then*. But just this one time she wanted all the credit. Just this one time she wanted to prove that she could do it without any help.

Ace moved even closer, and the scent of fresh soap and aftershave drifted over. Another glance at the unyielding look on his face told her that there was no sense in arguing with him. He was determined to keep the ring, and she didn't want to start the night off at odds. That could jeopardize the mission, which she wouldn't do for anything, even if it meant that she didn't get sole credit for the capture. Still, there might be another way.

She sidled even closer to Ace, her eyes darting to his pocket again. Darn. Being this close to the man sure was distracting. Maybe she should rethink her vow to not pick things up with Ace where they'd left off. *After* this mission.

A pang of guilt stabbed her as she cuddled into

him. It sure did feel good, and so what if she had ulterior motives? She might as well enjoy herself too. Ace dropped his hand to her bare shoulder and rubbed small circles on her skin, making her shiver.

"Kate. Please talk to me. Please tell me how I can fix this between us." He sounded so sweet and eager and earnest that she couldn't resist looking at him again. Big mistake. He'd leaned in, putting their lips only inches apart. "Please. Tell me what I can do to win you back. You're all I've ever wanted."

"I-I am?" she whispered, her gaze dropping to his lips before meeting his eyes again. She forced her thoughts to the ring in his pocket. If she could just distract him.

His warm, minty breath fanned her face and his free hand cupped her cheek, his thumb stroking her cheekbone so softly, tenderly. She was hypnotized, caught in his spell, ready and willing to go along with anything he suggested.

"Tell me, Kate." Ace moved closer, only millimeters away now. "Tell me what I can do."

In answer, she pressed her lips to his. As always, the connection between them flared, swirling through her overtaxed mind and blotting out everything and causing time to stand still.

As his lips brushed over hers, Kate tried to

remember why she was here, what she was doing. Oh right, the ring. Her hands trailed up his chest, felt the lump of the receiver ring, and slipped inside to steal it before she could have second thoughts. Then she locked her arms around Ace's neck and kissed him back for all she was worth.

When they finally broke apart he looked as flustered as she felt.

Ace ran his hands through his hair and then stood, offering his hand to help her up. Kate at least had the presence of mind to slip the ring inside the front of her dress when he wasn't looking. She followed him out the door. Her lips were tingling and her heart pounded. She had the ring and The Lemur was within her grasp. So why was it all she could think about was what the heck she was going to do about her feelings for Ace once all this was over?

ACE WALKED beside Kate down the hall leading to the stairs up to the main deck. He would've liked to keep that kiss going, but he wouldn't push her. He'd worked too hard to get back to this point with her, and he refused to blow it now.

They emerged topside to find the yacht a flurry of

activity. Sal and Gertie, and even Benny, alongside Vic and Carlotta, were setting up the dining area for the reception. Gertie and Sal were, of course, arguing about what went where, and Kate's mother was trying to smooth things over.

Kate veered off toward Carlotta and Gertie while Ace headed for Vic. They were anchored just off the port of Venice, and he wanted to make sure all the details were covered.

"You ready?" he asked Vic as he helped move a buffet table into place.

"Yeah, I'm ready." Vic stepped back and eyed the row of linen-covered tables to make sure they were straight. Satisfied, he faced Ace. "My daughter's going to be upset if you nab this thief without her, you know."

"Yeah, I know." Ace smiled. Couldn't help it. Kate had thought she'd been so clever down in their suite, but he'd felt the brush of her fingers near his pocket and knew the truth. "That's why I let her steal the receiver ring from me. If you spot The Lemur, you'll be telling Kate, not me. She'll catch the thief this time."

"Hmm." Vic didn't look happy. "What if this person's dangerous? We already know he's smart. They've eluded capture for years."

"That's why I'm taking extra precautions." Ace lifted the edge of his tuxedo jacket to reveal a small pistol in a holster beneath his arm. "I won't let anything happen to Kate. I promise."

Vic smiled, a twinkle in his eyes as he clapped Ace on the back. "You're a good man. I'll be extra vigilant too. Promise." Then he stepped away, his expression turning serious. "Kate's still my little girl. I want her taken care of properly."

"Understood." Ace didn't hesitate. He wanted nothing more than to protect Kate for the rest of his life, if she'd let him. He also knew how important proving that she could capture The Lemur on her own was to her, and he wanted her to have that victory. After that, he'd put his plan to get back together into full force. He started to respond to Vic, only to be cut off by a dazzling spray of fireworks erupting in the sky over the docks ahead. Ace checked his watch then nodded to Vic. "Show time."

Chapter Twelve

K ate stood on the deck of The Leviathan and watched crowds of wealthy, well-dressed guests board the ship. Already the air was rife with chatter and the sound of clinking glasses and the smells of liquor, champagne, and bacon-wrapped scallops. Still, she kept an eye on her two main suspects, Ned and Penny. If either made a move toward the stairs leading below, she'd be ready.

Gertie, dressed in the wait staff outfit of crisp white shirt, black pants and vest, strolled through the crowd, balancing a tray of drinks. She slowed as she passed Kate and turned her back, pretending to look out over the scenery as she whispered, "All systems go. The eagle is still in place." Then she glided off to serve drinks to a crowd of bejeweled, over-the -hill wives of art patrons.

Gertie could be so dramatic sometimes. She'd insisted on using the code phrase to indicate that the painting was still in place. That way Kate would know that The Lemur had not yet made his move. Kate's nerves zinged in anticipation. The Lemur would have to make his move soon.

Laughter bubbled up from behind Kate, and she turned to see Alexis Pennington acting her usual flirty self, dressed in a skintight floor-length gown that Kate was surprised she could even walk in. Alexis flitted from one man to another, laughing a bit too loud and smiling a bit too wide, all the while casting glances up at the bridge. Trying to make Benny jealous? Or was she keeping an eye out for something else, perhaps trying to judge the best time to sneak below and steal the painting?

As she waited, Kate slipped the receiver ring out from where she'd tucked it inside her bra and slipped it on her finger. Ace was not anywhere around to see it, and if he did by some miracle spot it she'd explain it away somehow. Distracted, Kate made her way through the crowds, greeting those people she — as Connie Carlson — knew and introducing herself to those she didn't. She used her country bumpkin accent and manners while keeping one eye on the interior stairs leading below decks and the other trying to spot her ever-elusive boss among the knots of guests.

If only the stupid ring would vibrate already so she could get this over with and Max could see just how competent she was.

Up ahead, Kate spotted the back of a tall, dark-haired man. She'd only ever seen Max from behind, but that sure looked like him. Forgetting her post for a moment, Kate darted through the clusters of people nearby to reach him. But when she got there, he was gone.

Darn it.

Disappointed, Kate glanced around and spotted the same man ducking inside toward the bar. Mercedes wasn't far behind. That had to be Max. Kate took off again, realizing belatedly that she and Mercedes were wearing the same gown. How could that be a coincidence? She was sure it wasn't. Had Gideon told Mercedes what Kate was wearing? No, he wouldn't do that, not unless Mercedes had a method of wheedling information out of him. Then again, maybe she had. And darn it all, did Mercedes actually look better in the gown than Kate did?

She elbowed her way to the entrance to the bar area and peered through the crowd. Max stood at the bar, Mercedes on one side and Alexis Pennington of all people on the other, flirting and hanging on his arm. He faced Alexis, so all Kate could see was the back of his head. Darn it!

She was pushing her way through the crowd at the door toward the bar when the high-pitched squeal of a microphone screeched through the air, followed by a *tap-tap*. Soon, Ace's voice surrounded her again — deep, rich, slightly rough — and a small thrill went through her despite her earlier resolve.

She pivoted to face the front of the main lounge. Was it time for the presentation already? No need to battle the bar crowd then; she'd see Max when they handed over the painting.

"Attention, ladies and gentleman," Ace said over the sound system. "Roger Conway here. On behalf of myself and my beautiful wife, Connie." He paused, catching Kate's eye and winking. "We'd like to welcome you aboard our lovely new yacht, The Leviathan. If I may ask my wife to join me, we'll get started with the presentation. Come on up here, Schmoopums."

Ughh. There he goes with the pet names again. So annoying.

Kate smoothed a hand down her beaded dress and started forward, only to feel the ring vibrate on her hand. She stopped beside Alexis and stared at her hand.

Crap!

Indecision paralyzed her. This could be her one chance to catch The Lemur. But if she ran downstairs now she'd disturb the presentation, miss seeing Max in person, and probably piss off Ace.

She turned and bolted for the stairs. She couldn't let The Lemur get away, not after all the expense and trouble Max had gone to.

Ace's voice followed her. "Connie? Sweetie-eatums ... where did you run off to? Oh, well, uh, okay. It looks like my wife might be otherwise occupied for a moment, so I'll continue on solo."

Applause erupted as Ace started his spiel about Max and his foundation and the Ritzholdt Museum while Kate hurried into the bar area and the stairs leading below deck. She unhooked the maroon velvet rope strung there to keep nosy guests out, then refastened it behind her.

Kate took a last glance around the crowd. Which guest hadn't she seen in a while? Alexis had been right near her when the ring went off. She'd seen Sinclair groping someone shortly before that. And hadn't she seen Penny at the bar? But she hadn't seen Ned in quite a while.

She crept downstairs slowly, careful not to make any noise. When she reached the bottom she peered around the corner and spotted a black-tuxedo-clad figure turning the corner into the side hallway. At least she thought it was a tux. Hard to tell in the dim lights and shadows. Where was her father? Kate made her way toward the storeroom, wishing she'd brought her weapon, but there was nowhere to hide a holster beneath her skintight gown.

The storeroom door was cracked open. Her pulse kicked up a notch. Okay. Time to catch a thief. Cautiously, Kate nudged the door open and leaned inside, expecting to catch Ned with the painting in his hands and —.

Pain burst through the back of her head, and white stars peppered her vision. As Kate fell to the floor, her last thoughts were that she'd fallen for the oldest trick. The room was empty. The thief had doubled back and knocked her out from behind. And the worst part was she hadn't even seen who it was.

Chapter Thirteen

Kate blinked her eyes open to find Penny leaning over her, her blue eyes concerned. No, wait. Something wasn't right. Trying to force her dizzy, aching head to clear, Kate did her best to concentrate. Had Penny hit her? But if Penny was The Lemur, why would she stick around?

Wait. That's what was wrong. Penny had brown eyes, not blue. At least that's what color they were earlier at the pool when she'd gotten something in her eye. Kate scowled. Could she have been wearing contacts like Kate? Why?

There could be only one reason someone would wear a disguise.

Scrambling to unsteady feet, Kate swayed a bit before pointing a finger at Penny. "You! You're The Lemur. I caught you!"

"What? No." Penny snorted. "I'm not The Lemur. *You* are. And I caught you!"

"You didn't catch anyone. Certainly not me." Kate rubbed her throbbing temple and shook her fuzzy head, the wig skewing sideways.

"Aha! I knew you were in disguise." Penny whipped out her phone. "Just stay there while I call the authorities."

Kate grabbed the phone. "I'm not the only one in disguise. Your eyes were brown earlier. Explain that!"

Penny's back straightened, and her features sharpened into a look of self-importance. "I'm undercover. On a special mission from the Goolenhem Museum to catch The Lemur. That would be *you*. I saw through that phony Connie and Roger Carlson act on day one. So tell me, where are all the stolen paintings?"

Kate's gaze narrowed, and she shoved the phone behind her back. What kind of a fast one was Penny trying to pull? If the Goolenhem Museum had an agent like Kate she would know, wouldn't she? Then again, Kate's identity was kept secret from the outside world for obvious reasons, so it was possible Penny was telling the truth.

"I don't believe you. I'm the one undercover here. From the *Ritzholdt* Museum!"

"Prove it!"

"*You* prove it!"

The two women stood glaring at each other, hands on hips, each challenging the other to go first.

"Ladies, ladies. What is going on here?" Ace asked, coming up behind Penny.

Kate swayed slightly and Ace was at her side in an instant, his arms around her, supporting her. For a moment, Kate wanted to just sag against him and let him take over. But she had a thief to catch and a point to make. She straightened and pushed away from him.

"What's happening here?" he asked, his gaze running over her flushed face and crooked wig. "Are you all right?"

"No. I'm not. She hit me over the head and stole the painting." Kate pointed to Penny. "Arrest her!"

Ace glanced at Penny and drew his gun.

"Hey, wait a minute," Penny said, backing up with her hands in the air. "I didn't hit anybody. And I didn't steal anything. I came down here to check on the storeroom and found your wife or partner or whatever she is lying there, out cold."

"Why would you be checking on the storeroom?" Ace asked, unconvinced.

"Because I thought you two were The Lemur."

Penny sniffed. "As I was just telling *Connie* over here, I'm undercover to catch the thief."

Ace holstered his gun. "Do you have proof that you're undercover?"

Penny signed and reached into her bra, producing a laminated card containing a photo of a slightly different-looking Penny with the name Wanda Deavers and a museum emblem and watermark. It looked official.

"Looks like the real thing." Ace handed it back. "But what are you doing here?"

"The Goolenhem has been after The Lemur for six years now. He's stolen several items, and we want them back. Or for him to stop. When the big bosses heard about this new couple buying up artwork and having the special cruise, they figured The Lemur would be on board. Once I saw your pathetic disguises, I figured *you* two were The Lemur. Can you prove otherwise?"

Kate glanced at Ace. She didn't have room in her outfit for credentials, but Ace did. He pulled them out of his breast pocket and handed them over. They must have satisfied Penny — Wanda — because she sighed, handed them back and said. "Great. So this is all a setup?"

Kate nodded. "To flush out The Lemur."

"But a painting really is in the storeroom for him to steal. I saw it myself when I broke in last night to verify you were actually transporting it."

Kate cursed under her breath. "Guess that explains the ink on her hands."

Penny looked at her hands. "What ink?"

"The painting is a fake," Ace said. "We had the lock on the door and the safe painted with a special dye that only shows up under glasses designed to see it. We checked at the party last night and found both you and Ned had the dye on your hands."

Penny crossed her arms over her chest. "Well, since we've just established that none of us are actually The Lemur, I guess that narrows the field."

Ace met Kate's gaze as they both reached the same conclusion.

"Ned!" Kate said, taking off down the hall, not quite as steady as before.

Chapter Fourteen

Ace raced upstairs behind Kate, keeping a close eye on her. She seemed okay, but her normally graceful movements were a bit shaky, and he didn't like the paleness of her cheeks. Plus, she hadn't even tried to hide the receiver ring on her finger. Not that he cared, but it wasn't like her.

They found Ned sitting at the bar, calm as could be. The guy must be a pretty cool customer if he could sit there and pretend he hadn't just stolen what he believed to be a multi-million-dollar painting. Ace snorted. Ned wasn't even trying to escape, but that was probably part of his plan. Try not to attract attention and then simply walk off the ship. Well, we'll see about that.

Weaving through the crowds of guests sipping

drinks and nibbling appetizers, Ace and Kate made their way over to Ned at the bar.

"Where's your father?" Ace whispered close to Kate's ear. "I haven't seen Vic since set-up."

Why hadn't Vic been downstairs when Kate got clobbered? It wasn't like him to leave his post, especially when his daughter's safety was at stake. Had Ned done something to him?

"I'm not sure." She frowned, side-stepping to avoid Captain Benny's rotund form dancing with a female guest. "Now that you mention it, I didn't see him in the hallway downstairs when I went down there to follow Ned or Penny or whoever it was I followed."

"Dammit, he should've been there," Ace grumbled. "If he were, you might not have gotten hurt."

"I'm fine," she hissed between her teeth. "Ready?"

Ace felt anything but ready, but gave a curt nod anyway.

They stepped in front of Ned, effectively blocking him in on his stool. Kate crossed her arms and narrowed her gaze. "Mind telling us where the painting is, Mr. Parsons?"

"Excuse me?" he sputtered, choking on his drink. "What the hell are you talking about?"

"The painting. Downstairs in the storage room," Ace said, straightening to his full height for full intimidation. "We know you stole it, Parsons. Or maybe we should call you The Lemur."

"Oh, that's rich!" Ned glared at them. "Especially coming from you, Roger. You deal in black-market paintings. Who are you to accuse me of anything?"

"We know you were in the storage room downstairs, Ned. We marked the door with special ink that showed up on your hands." Kate exhaled slowly. Her slight wobble caused Ace concern, but he had to focus on making sure Ned was caught with the painting and arrested. There was no way Kate was going to just sit down and miss out on all the fun. "Give it up, Ned. We want the painting and we want it now."

A small muscle ticked near Ned's tight jaw. He set his drink on the bar and blinked several times before answering. "Okay, fine. Yes, I have been down in that storage room, but not for the reason you think. I came on this cruise because my great-great-grandfather was Otto Smythefeldt."

He said the name as though Ace and Kate should recognize it, but Ace didn't. A glance at Kate told him she was confused as well.

Ned gave an exasperated sigh at their silence.

"Otto was a wealthy Jewish businessman in Berlin before World War II. The Nazis stole most of the artwork and valuables from his home during the war. I've spent the last five years scouring the art circuit looking to recover what items I could for my family." He reached into his tuxedo jacket pocket and pulled out a small bundle of photographs. "I've even got photos of the artworks and provenance to prove my legitimate claim."

The photos looked real enough to Ace. Some of them showed an old man, presumably Otto, standing near various paintings. Others were of sales receipts and other documentation to prove that Otto had owned the artwork.

"So that's why I was downstairs in that storeroom and I guess that must be why I had your special ink on my hands. Though I have to say I never saw anything on my hands." Ned looked down at his hands. "I tried to pick the lock last night, but was interrupted, so I had to go back in tonight. I only wanted to look at the painting, to see for myself whether it was mine or not. If it was mine, I would have confronted you and asked that it be returned. I'd never steal it. That's what got my family into this mess to begin with."

"If you didn't take it, why did you run?" Kate asked.

"I heard someone coming down the hallway and figured it was best if I didn't get caught in the room."

Kate turned to face Ace. "He must have heard my father. Or me. If what he says is true, he's not our guy. And we've ruled out Penny too."

Ace's phone buzzed in his pocket.

"Looks like phone service is back," Ned said, still sitting calmly. If this guy was The Lemur he had nerves of titanium. But Ace didn't think he was. The guy was too jittery normally. It was more likely his story was true. He checked his phone. It was Vic.

"Hey, Ace, I chased a guy down the hall down here a little while ago. He got away, man. Sorry about that," Vic said.

"Was it Ned?" Ace asked, his eyes still pinned on the man on the stool in front of him.

"Yeah, think so. I think he was in the storage room, because when I came back the lock had been picked and the door was open."

"Uh huh. Can you go in and check on the painting?"

"Sure thing." There was silence for a few seconds, followed by Vic coming back on. "Hey, great news.

The painting is still there, so it looks like we might still have a chance to catch this guy. You want me to lock it up again?"

"That would be great." Ace clicked off and turned to Kate to relay what Vic had told him.

"It's still there?" Kate cast a doubtful glance at Ned. "But the reception is almost over. The Lemur should have struck by now."

Ace put a consoling hand on her shoulder. "I know. I hate to say it, but it looks like The Lemur didn't fall for our bait after all."

KATE WAS in no mood for Ace to fawn over her the way he was now. Another time, maybe, but right now she had a monster headache and a raging case of disappointment over not catching The Lemur. It was kind of cute the way he'd pulled her outside to the fresh air on the deck away from everyone and gotten her some ice water, but Kate was too angry to fully appreciate it.

Kate took a swallow of her water and did her best not to be annoyed with Ace. It wasn't his fault the thief hadn't made a play for the painting as they'd expected. And he was being sweet to her. The light caught the fake engagement ring on her finger and reminded her of the receiver ring she'd stolen from him. Where was it? She hadn't noticed in all the excitement, but it was no longer on her finger. Had it fallen off in the scuffle with Penny? She'd better go back and get it before Ace noticed it missing. Come to think of it, why hadn't he noticed that already?

Ace's phone jangled from the pocket of his tuxedo, and he pulled it out and set it on the bar when Mercedes's name popped up on the caller ID. Glancing around to make sure no one was within hearing range, he hit speaker phone and dialed down the volume.

"Hey, Mercy," Ace said. "Where are you guys?"

"Back on board the Maximum Quest already," she said, her tone clipped. "Max was hoping we'd have The Lemur on board with us, to take to the police. But because that's not going to happen and your mission failed, we'll be leaving shortly."

Kate winced. "We haven't failed. It's not our fault if The Lemur didn't make his move."

"Exactly," a deep masculine voice, tinged with a hint of accent, said over the line. *Max.* Irish or British, it didn't matter. That voice got Kate every time. Her knees went wobbly. It was a good thing she was sitting, because she might've melted into a puddle of goo otherwise. "Neither of you should feel disappointed or blame yourselves. You both did the best you could."

"Can't you stay a bit longer?" Kate asked, still hoping for a glimpse of her elusive boss. "Maybe come back on deck of The Leviathan for a farewell drink?"

"Sorry, Kate. Alas, I have pressing business in Rome tomorrow," he said. "Ace, be sure that all the loose ends are tied up on this mission before you head back to the mainland."

Kate scowled and pushed to her feet. Clearly Max thought of Ace as the leader of this mission, and that only served to put her in an even worse mood. Needing some space, she ignored Ace's questioning look and headed toward the bow to stare down at the Maximum Quest docked nearby. The ship was a smaller cruiser, and she could just make out Max's back as he strolled inside the bridge of the ship and out of sight. Mercedes wasn't far behind. She glanced Kate's way and gave a two-finger wave. Even though she wasn't close enough to see it, Kate imagined the annoying assistant's smirk.

Shoulders slumped, Kate turned away to face the

party again. She was zero for two for the night — no Lemur and no sighting of Max. The only positive thing was she could ditch this stupid costume. She reached up to scratch beneath her wig and realized it was crooked. Kate straightened the dumb thing, then rubbed her nose. A few of the guests were leaving now, disembarking to head back to their own private yachts, speedboats, or limos. Soon they would clean up the mess and call the mission over. A failure.

Ace came up beside her. "Sorry things didn't work out like you wanted," he said, leaning against the railing. "I'm sure you're disappointed."

Exhaling slowly, Kate looked out at the lights of Venice. The sound of the water lapping and the sight of gondolas and boats moving in and out of the canals soothed her. Maybe she'd take a little vacation in Venice now that she was already here. That way the trip wouldn't be a total loss. Maybe she'd even ask Ace to join her. "I am disappointed, but you shouldn't be sorry. None of this was your fault."

He took her hand and smiled, then frowned. "Where's the receiver ring?"

"Huh?" She narrowed her gaze. "Wait. You knew I took it?"

Ace shrugged. "Yeah, I felt you take it from my pocket. But I figured you needed it more than I did.

Besides, it didn't really matter to me which of us caught the thief as long as justice was done."

And there it was. Just when she got to thinking things might work out between them he went and did something like this. He'd *let* her steal the ring. Was he going to *let* her catch The Lemur too? Didn't he understand that she wanted to do it all on her own?

Kate snatched her hand back. "Well, that's just dandy. In case you haven't noticed, I don't need your help." She turned to head back inside. "Now if you'll excuse me, I need to go find the ring. I'm sure Gideon will want it. At least *he* knows the right way to help a girl catch a thief!"

Kate marched through the open glass sliders into the main salon, jostling through the throng of party-goers who were still milling around, getting their fill of the free cocktails and hors d'oeuvres.

To her dismay, Ace followed close behind her. "Wait up Kate ... er ... Connie. I didn't mean to upset you."

"Forget it," Kate shot over her shoulder without looking back. "I should have known not to expect more."

"Hey, wait. I've tried everything I know. Come on, Wookie Oookums, don't be angry."

The pleading note in Ace's voice made her falter

for a second. She didn't dare turn around and look at him for fear the sad apologetic look on his face would melt her heart. Instead, she turned down the hallway to the stairs that led below, yelling over her shoulder, "And stop calling me those stupid pet names!"

Chapter Fifteen

Kate's anger had cooled a little by the time they got to the storage room, so she grudgingly let Ace help her look for the ring. They were on their hands and knees in the doorway when Gertie happened by on her way to put the vacuum back in the closet.

"What are you folks doing? Is that some new kind of sex thing?"

Kate snorted. "Hardly. We're looking for that ring Gideon sent in the gadgets bag. I lost it in my struggle with Penny. Wanda. Whomever."

Gertie dropped to her knees and started helping. "Yeah, sorry I heard the painting never got stolen. There're still guests on board, though. And they sure are making a mess. Maybe we're giving up too soon."

Black dress shoes came into Kate's line of vision,

and she looked up to see Benny looking down at them, a quizzical look on his face.

"What are you people doing? Is that some new kind of sex thing?" Benny asked.

Gertie scowled up at him. "Ha! You would know about that, with your new girlfriend."

Benny flushed.

"We're looking for the ring Gideon gave us." Kate crawled further into the room to search the corners.

"But won't you guys scare off The Lemur if he comes down to get the painting?" Benny asked.

"Doubt it." Ace straightened and held up the ring. "Everyone will be off the ship soon. The crowd is already thinning. If The Lemur was going to strike he would have done it by now."

Gertie stood, knees creaking. "Then I guess you won't be needing my painting anymore. Mind if I take it?"

Kate and Ace glanced at each other and shrugged.

"Don't see why not." Kate gestured toward the pallet that the painting had been stored in, and Gertie walked over and carefully took it out. She held it up, a smile on her face.

"Yeah, this was one of my best works." Suddenly her smile turned to a frown. She pulled the painting to within an inch of her face. "Hey wait a minute! This isn't my painting."

Kate moved to her side. "What do you mean? Looks exactly like it to me."

Gertie looked at her as if she were crazy. "Are you kidding? This isn't as finely detailed. Look at the horse and that ear. But the real tell is right here." Gertie tapped her finger on the bottom left corner of the canvas.

"I don't see anything," Ace said.

"Yeah, that's the problem. I always put in a little something extra on all my fakes to identify them as mine. This time it was a little brown rabbit in the left-hand corner. No rabbit on this one. Not at all."

"Doesn't that beat all," Benny said. "What in the world happened to your painting, and who put this one in here?"

Kate's eyes met Ace's as realization dawned. "The Lemur must have taken it! He made a fake to throw us off track. Makes perfect sense. The Lemur figured Roger and Connie wouldn't know a fake from the real thing, so he could steal what he thought was the real Picasso and we'd never even know we'd been robbed."

"But who?" Ace asked. "We know it wasn't Penny or Ned."

"It couldn't have been Sinclair either. I saw him upstairs all night groping the guests," Kate said.

"It has to be Alexis," Ace said. "I didn't want to believe it was her at first because she seemed too flighty. But it has to be her. She's the only one left who had ink on her hands, right?"

Kate snapped her fingers. "And she had paint on the collar of her cover-up the other day on deck. At first I thought it was Dottie's nail polish. She must have broken into the room that night to look at the painting so she could replace it with a fake. Then she came back tonight and switched them!"

"That explains why she was always late and running around after Dottie. She was in her room the whole time painting." Ace turned to Gertie. "Did you see any paintings in there?"

Gertie shook her head. "Their room was a mess. But the safe ... she might have kept it in there."

Kate turned to Benny. "Where is she now?"

"She said she was going to pack and then sit at the bar for a few last cocktails before we ... er ... she disembarked." Benny's voice was uncertain. "But I don't think it could be her —."

"C'mon!" Kate grabbed Ace's arm. "We need to get to her before she disappears if we want to catch her red-handed."

Chapter Sixteen

S al raised a brow at them from behind the bar as they skidded into the room. The bar area was still crowded with guests sipping ice-laden cocktails, the sounds of conversation and clinking glasses permeating the room even though the reception was winding down.

"What's wrong?" Sal asked as they approached the bar.

"Where is Alexis?" Ace asked.

Gertie rushed in behind them. "Hey, can you guys slow down? Those stairs are hard on an old lady's knees."

"You didn't have to follow us, Gertie. We've got it covered," Ace said.

"Hell with that. I want to find the painting. That's

my best work, and I want it back." Gertie turned to Sal. "Now where in Hades is Alexis?"

"I'm not sure. Poor Dottie was in here all upset that Alexis told her to find her own way home." Sal leaned across the bar and lowered his voice. "I felt so bad for her that I gave her a bottle of Stoliano. You know, that liqueur she likes? Drinks it on the rocks. We had one brand-new in the box that we hadn't cracked open, so I figured it'd be no harm."

"Where's Dottie now?" Kate asked.

Sal shrugged. "Took the bottle to her room and said she might try to catch her niece before she ran off." Sal got a thoughtful look on his face. "Do you think she was running off with Benny? And what's the rush anyway? Ain't the mission over?"

Kate was already rushing off before Sal even got the sentence out of his mouth. If they wanted to catch The Lemur they had to hurry. Alexis could still be packing, but after she was off the boat their odds of catching her were slim.

Kate's heart galloped as they ran through the crowd, jostling elbows and spilling drinks. Kate ignored the yells of "Hey!" and "Watch it!" as they burst into the hallway, taking the stairs to the rooms below two at a time.

Alexis's door was closed. Ace tried the knob, but it was locked.

"Try Dottie's door. It's an adjoining room. She's probably still here." Kate rushed to the next door, but that was locked too.

"You think she's hiding inside or already gone?" Ace asked.

"I don't know. But it would be clever to hide inside the room while we go on a wild goose chase through Venice."

"Right." Ace stepped back as far as he could, then charged for the door with his shoulder in the lead.

"Oh for crying out loud, I've got the keys." Gertie came huffing down the hallway dangling the room keys in her hand. "One of the advantages of being the maid."

Gertie shoved the door open, and they piled inside.

The room appeared empty. The shade over the porthole window was drawn, the bedclothes a messy heap on the bed, and the caustic smell of nail polish remover permeated the air.

Ace rushed into the adjoining room while Kate checked the bathroom.

"No one is here. They're both gone." Kate's shoulders weighed heavy with disappointment. If Alexis had gotten off the boat she could be anywhere by now.

"They sure did leave this room messy." Gertie got down on the floor and lifted the bed skirt to look under the bed. "I mean, I knew they were slobs because I had to come in and clean. I never suspected Alexis was painting a reproduction. I thought all those smudges on the vanity were nail polish."

Kate sniffed the air. "Yeah that smell must be turpentine. Smells just like nail polish remover."

Gertie raised her nose and sniffed. "Nah, that *is* nail polish remover. Alexis must have used acrylic paints. You can tell that painting wasn't done in quality oils like mine. Oils take too long to dry, and Alexis wouldn't have had that kind of time on this trip. She must have taken a photo of it the first night, then spent the rest of the time painting. She switched them at the party tonight."

"Right. At the party... " Kate frowned and turned from the closet she was inspecting back to Gertie. "Wait a minute. Didn't you say that you checked the storage room and the painting was there before the presentation? You remember, you used the code about the eagle."

"Yeah, it was there."

"Did you look closely at it? I mean to determine whether it was your painting or the reproduction?"

Gertie flushed. "Okay, fine, I admit I did pull it out to admire it. So sue me. It's one of my best and I like looking at it." Her shoulders slumped. "And now it's gone."

"How long between when you saw the painting and then gave me the code signal?" Kate asked.

"Couldn't have been more than five minutes. I had changed into this wait staff getup and then I swung by the storage room and came right up and got my first tray of booze. Saw you only a second later."

Kate turned to Ace. "Something doesn't add up. I saw Alexis at the party myself when I talked to Gertie. And she was in the bar flirting with Max right before the ring went off. She wouldn't have had time to go downstairs, exchange the paintings, and then hide the real one back in her cabin. And she was wearing a tight dress, so no way she could have hidden the painting in there."

Gertie fished a thin bottle of booze out of the trash can — the Stoliano that Dottie favored. "I don't know about any of that, but who would toss out this booze? It's a perfectly good bottle. In fact, I think I need a drink after all this."

"Is that the bottle that Sal gave Dottie?" Kate glanced into the trash can. Something else was in there.

Kate fished out a pair of black elbow-length gloves. The same gloves Dottie had worn the previous day. The day they'd put the dye on the lock and safe. Kate closed her eyes and remembered. Dottie had had them on earlier, but not later when they'd been looking at the guests' hands with the special glasses. She'd bet good money now that those gloves were covered in dye.

Her stomach knotted. She'd been kind to Dottie, feeling sorry for her at the pool because she'd messed up her nails. But that wasn't nail polish, Kate realized now. It was acrylic paint.

Gertie tipped the large bottle up to her mouth again and Kate glanced around the room for the box it came in. Sal had said he had given Dottie the bottle in the box. The box was the perfect height in which to hide the rolled up painting. And the box was nowhere to be found.

Dottie was The Lemur!

"What is it?" Ace's narrowed eyes were full of questions. "I know that look. You figured something out, didn't you?"

"I did. Alexis isn't the Lemur. Dottie is."

"What?" Gertie and Ace asked at the same time.

Kate didn't have time to explain, she had a killer to catch. She was already halfway out the door, yelling over her shoulder. "She wasn't as senile as we thought. Getting lost was all an act so she could have an excuse to be near the storage room. And now she's getting away!"

Kate raced up the stairs to the ship railing. Her eyes scanned the crowd milling on the dock in their evening gowns and tuxes. Some brandished full champagne glasses, the golden bubbly liquid spilling over the sides as they stepped aboard their own yachts.

At the far end of the dock she spotted Dottie climbing into a lone waiting water taxi, the long narrow cardboard box of the Stoliano bottle tucked possessively under her arm.

Chapter Seventeen

Without waiting for Ace, Kate took off down the gangway and rushed out onto the dock, dodging the people in her way, yelling all the while for the water taxi to wait. She saw Dottie lean forward and whisper something to the driver. He turned and locked eyes with Kate, then revved the taxi's engine, and the boat sped down the Grand Canal at a good clip, a rooster tail spewing up in its wake.

Kate tottered on the stilettos, her feet already aching. The heels! Gideon was a genius. She half hopped on one foot then the other, snapping off the heel and trying not to slow her pursuit while keeping her eye on the water taxi the whole time. The flatter shoes were much more comfortable, and she picked up speed.

Ahead were a few more water taxis. She tried to

hail one, but they all appeared to be occupied. Great! Kate kept running, spotting Dottie's boat turning down one of the narrower canals.

Tall buildings crowded her on either side as she drew deeper into Venice, the ancient architecture a maze of brick and stone. Her footsteps echoed off the buildings, mingling with the sound of water lapping the sides of the canal.

Winded, she stopped to catch her breath. How was she going to navigate these narrow streets to head Dottie off on the canal? The bracelet! She ripped it off her wrist and, sure enough, a small map of the streets and waters of Venice was engraved inside. She was going to recommend Gideon for a raise. Right after she caught The Lemur.

According to Gideon's graphics, if she cut down the alley to her right then made a left at the next intersection, she should be able to zig-zag back over to Dottie's canal and cut her off. She clicked the back of one of her earrings and prayed Benny would pick up her signal and send reinforcements in time. Maybe not Ace, though, at least until she had The Lemur under arrest, but she'd welcome the rest of the Golden Capers gang.

After a few deep breaths, Kate took off again, following the route indicated by the bracelet. She darted out onto the sidewalk beside the canal in time to see Dottie's taxi veer left onto an intersecting canal. Unfortunately, she was on the wrong side of the water, and there was no bridge in sight. Now what? She couldn't swim, and the canal was crowded with gondolas.

Gondolas!

Kate summoned the nearest one and climbed aboard, talking loudly to be heard over the accordion player in the back of the boat. "Can you catch up to the water taxi that just turned over there?"

The gondolier smiled at her, his English broken as he asked, "Does pretty lady want a ride?"

"No, no." She pointed to where Dottie's taxi had disappeared. "I need you to follow that boat. Per favore! Follow. That. Boat." She made hand gestures that would hopefully translate. "*Capisci?*"

The man in the back sped up the accordion playing. "Music?"

Kate shook her head and jabbed her finger in Dottie's direction again. "No. Um." Dang. What was the word for follow? "*Fausto!*"

The gondolier stared at her blankly and shrugged. The accordion player frowned and switched to a different, more ominous, tune. The tune was fitting given the situation, but Kate didn't much care to listen to music.

Crap! Maybe she *should* have taken those Italian lessons her mother had suggested. But there was no time to sit around trying to explain what she wanted.

Kate spun around, looking for another gondolier, preferably one who spoke English. But all the gondolas appeared to be occupied.

She looked to the other canal, where she could just see the back of Dottie's water taxi disappearing. The Lemur was getting away. Kate would have to do something drastic.

The waterway was crowded with gondolas, the gondoliers in their striped shirts and happy smiles standing in back, paddling sight-seeing tourists slowly along the canal.

A gondola glided close, sparking an idea. Maybe she couldn't swim to the other side, but there was another way to get across.

Kate stood on the seat, much to the dismay of the gondolier, held her breath, and jumped onto the passing gondola. The happy passengers—perhaps honeymooners judging by the serene smiles on their faces before Kate thumped into their boat—jumped when she startled them out of their reverie.

THE ACCORDION PLAYER SQUEEZED HARD, a loud note cutting the air.

"I'm so sorry," Kate said to the couple. "Just passing through."

She stood at the ready. Another gondola was coming, and a third approached from the opposite direction. If she timed it right, she could leapfrog across the gondolas to the other side.

The gondola passed alongside and Kate leapt, startling everyone on board. They were speechless staring at her, and by the time they found their voices Kate had already leapt onto the next gondola.

She continued on, each leap punctuated by a high note from the accordion above the angry shouts of the gondoliers and their passengers.

Kate didn't have time to stop and apologize. She made the final leap to the sidewalk and took off running, ignoring the angry cursing gondoliers and the accordion player — who was now playing *The Flight of the Bumble Bee* — as she raced toward the other canal.

Kate careened around the corner to see Dottie's water taxi taking a right into a side canal. A quick glance at her bracelet showed that canal led back out to the Grand Canal. If Dottie made it out there, Kate would never catch her.

Oh no, I'm not letting you get away, not when I'm so close!

Kate picked up speed, knocking into pedestrians as she raced along the sidewalk, taking a right onto the walkway lining the canal Dottie's taxi had taken.

Shoot! She could see the Grand Canal just a few blocks away. Dottie's boat was motoring down the middle of the side canal toward a lovely arched stone footbridge that spanned the canal just near the end before it dumped out into the Grand Canal.

Dottie glanced back at Kate with a scowl on her face. She leaned forward and said something to the driver.

Kate would never be able to jump onto Dottie's taxi. It was too far away in the middle of the canal and a moving target to boot. But Kate didn't give up easily.

She hauled ass to the footbridge, sprinting as hard as she could to surpass the boat. This was her one shot to catch The Lemur.

With seconds to spare, Kate raced up the center of the footbridge and clambered up onto the railing.

As the taxi roared underneath the bridge. Kate closed her eyes and jumped.

Chapter Eighteen

Kate landed in the water taxi with a bone-jarring thud. She gripped the edge of the boat until she got her bearings, glancing around to see Dottie coming at her with a bottle of raspberry liquor in her hand, brandishing it like a weapon. The older woman swung the heavy glass bottle toward Kate's head.

Apparently Dottie had a thing for tall liquor bottles. Had she had the water taxi stocked or had she pilfered it from Sal? This one wasn't as tall as the Stoliano, but it would make just as deadly a weapon.

She ducked in time and scurried to the other side of the small boat, all the while searching for something to use to defend herself. Gone was Dottie's ruse of frailty and senility. She swung that bottle like an Olympic hammer thrower.

THUNK!

The bottle came down hard on the boat's gunwale, shattering the glass. Raspberry liquor sprayed everywhere, covering both women in a sticky, sweet-smelling mess and leaving Dottie with a jagged hunk of glass to wield that was even more deadly than the intact bottle.

Scrambling to her feet, Kate blinked away the alcohol stinging her eyes and yelled for the taxi driver to stop.

"No!" Dottie shouted at the man. The boat teetered precariously as the women circled each other. The driver kept glancing back at them, his expression anxious. Dottie snarled. "You keep going and get me out of here or I'll never pay you the money I promised to help me escape. *Capisce?*"

"But what about the woman?" the driver asked in heavily accented English.

"Don't worry about her," Dottie said, her smile sinister. "I'll take care of her."

The engine roared and the water around them churned, spraying them again as they jetted out into the Grand Canal.

At least the spray helped rinse off some of the sticky raspberry, Kate thought absently as she tried to find a weakness in Dottie's defense. Best to keep her talking. Kate spotted the box holding the painting wedged beneath Dottie's seat and shook her head.

"So, it *was* you. You're The Lemur."

"That's right," Dottie said, no longer trying to hide her identity. "Good disguise, huh? No one ever suspects the little old lady. Got what I wanted, too."

"Did you?" Kate asked, cocking her head as she tried to calculate how to disarm Dottie. And then what? Hopefully Ace and the others were tracking her from the signal in her earring and would arrive soon. She glanced behind her but didn't see any boat zooming to the rescue. Looked like she'd have to do this all on her own. Wasn't that what she'd really wanted?

Kate turned back to Dottie. "I've got a surprise for you. That painting's a fake."

Dottie snorted. "Nice try. I know an original when I see one. You don't last as many years in the business as I have by being stupid."

"We hired one of the best forgers in the business. It was money well spent, I'd say." Kate flashed a sly smile. "Especially if it fooled a connoisseur like you. Or should I say *con artist*?"

"You're lying." Dottie raised her chin defiantly. "Hoping you'll get me to mess up, but you won't. I'm so close to escaping I can taste freedom. And I never lose a battle. I always get what I want."

"Go ahead." Kate widened her stance to keep her balance as the taxi driver swerved around another boat.

The Grand Canal was much wider than the side canals. Out here on the water highway they were surrounded by vessels of all sizes. Gondolas, taxis, yachts. Kate's heartbeat stumbled. If the driver wasn't careful he'd get them all killed. Blood pounding in her ears, Kate yelled to be heard above the roar of the engine. "Check the painting for yourself. There's a mark the forger puts on all her work. A sort of surprise to let the unlucky owners know they've been duped. See if you can find it."

For a moment, Dottie looked as though she wasn't going to check. Then she slowly inched backward, keeping her gaze locked on Kate, the jagged half bottle raised in front of her. With her free hand, Dottie reached down and grabbed the box, fumbling it open to snatch the rolled-up painting from inside.

Wind whipped around them as the driver zipped between obstacles ahead of them, and Kate's stomach lurched. The canvas flapped in the strong breeze, and Dottie's expression quickly morphed from one of gloating to disbelief. Kate couldn't help feeling a surge of victory. Guess The Lemur wasn't the big, bad art genius she thought she was.

"Is that a …" Dottie leaned closer and squinted. "Bunny rabbit?"

"Yep. Cute, isn't he?" Kate quipped.

With an angry snarl, Dottie tossed the fake painting aside and lunged at Kate, knocking them both sideways and to the deck. They rolled and wrestled in the sticky raspberry liquor, Kate struggling to avoid being skewered by the jagged bottle and Dottie doing her best to stab her.

Kate jumped up, trying to get leverage over Dottie, but the older woman had a good couple of inches on Kate and a few extra pounds. Kate soon found herself pressed to the gunwale of the boat, the shattered bottle hovering far too near her throat for comfort.

"You set me up!" Dottie hissed. "Nobody sets up The Lemur."

"We did," Kate squeaked as Dottie brought the glass closer. "You won't get away with this. I'm wearing a GPS tracker. Help is already on the way. They know where I am."

Kate glanced behind them again. Where were they?

"*Porca vacca!*" the Italian driver yelled, and

swerved sharply. The movement toppled Dottie to the side, allowing Kate to squirm out from under her. She'd no more than clambered to her feet, however, when Dottie was on her again.

The old lady was strong. She pushed Kate against the side of the boat, trying to topple her into the water. Kate pushed back, but it was hard to get leverage with her back bent over the gunwale.

The driver's curses escalated. Kate jerked her head toward the bow to see a massive yacht looming in front of them. Her eyes widened further when she read the name on the ship — the Maximum Quest. The cavalry had come, and they were heading straight for it.

"Turn!" Kate yelled. "We're going to smash into it!"

"Not me," Dottie said, grabbing the fake painting and tossing it over the side of the taxi. "I'm out of here."

"Oh, no you're not!" Kate rammed Dottie in the stomach with her shoulder, knocking the older woman down before racing to the front of the boat and shooing the driver out of the way. It was too late. She managed to alter their course only slightly as they raced toward the side of the Maximum Quest.

The boat seemed impossibly close as Kate jerked

the mahogany steering wheel. The water taxi veered as the side of the Maximum Quest blotted out everything else, and then ...

Smash!

The next few seconds were a blur. Time slowed as the wooden bow shattered, sending wood and splinters flying. Kate ducked, but not in time to stop a large chunk from slamming into the side of her head.

Darkness descended fast as she tumbled into the water along with Dottie and the driver. Debris floated all around them in the icy water. Kate battled to keep her eyes open, to swim upward, to stay conscious long enough to save herself. But she was so, so tired, and it wouldn't hurt to close her eyes just a moment, would it?

Her water-soaked dress felt like an anchor dragging her downward. Who knew rhinestones could be so heavy? Well, at least she'd still be dressed nice when they fished her body out. She only hoped the water wouldn't make it clingy in all the wrong places. She should just relax and surrender to blessed exhaustion and ...

Something hard and warm wrapped around her waist, hoisting her upward through the murky depths. Next thing she knew, her back was on a hard surface, her chest aching and her lungs heaving as she choked up water.

A shadowy figure bent over her, soothing her. Was it saying something? Kate heard only the sound of water swishing in her ears. And why couldn't she see clearly? She struggled to open her eyes. Wait, they *were* open. What the heck?

Kate shook her head, hoping to clear her vision. Her ears cleared up, and she heard a deep, Irish-accented voice trickling over her frayed nerves like warm honey. *Max.*

She shivered, coughed, and blinked hard as he leaned over her. Finally, her chance to see Max, but she couldn't see. The stupid fake eyelashes had clumped up and filled with water and were blurring her vision. She tried to sit up, but that made her dizzy and she fell back.

"Now, don't try to sit up. Everything will be fine," Max soothed. "And, Kate, good job. You caught The Lemur."

She tried to stay awake, really she did. But sleep beckoned and Kate was so very tired, and with the sound of Max's voice in her ears, she slipped into unconsciousness at last.

Chapter Nineteen

T*hree days later ... .*

"Can I get you another pillow, sweetie?" Gertie asked Kate, hovering around her chaise lounge. Most of the gang had doted over Kate for the better part of the week. The hit on the head in Venice had resulted in a mild concussion and she'd twisted her ankle pretty badly, but it was nothing that wouldn't mend. You'd think she was much worse off the way the Golden Capers gang mothered her. Then again, considering she was poolside at Golden Capers, enjoying a bit of R and R beneath the golden Florida sunshine, there were worse ways to spend an afternoon.

"No, thank you, Gertie. I'm fine." Kate took a sip of her fruity, non-alcoholic drink and smiled as the paper umbrella floating in it nudged her nose. Kate adjusted the lime-green pool towel underneath her, the movement sending the coconut scent of sunscreen wafting up. "Why don't you sit down and relax for a while?"

"Ugh. I wish." Gertie held her hand over her eyes and stared across the glimmering pool water to where Sal was making pina coladas in a blender at the tiki bar. Behind him, colorful party lights had been strung up along the tall fence ringing the pool. They were having a post-Lemur-capture celebration tonight. "Still got too much to do for the party."

She wandered away and Kate leaned back in her chair, setting her drink on the table beside her.

"Are you sure you're okay, dear?" her mother asked from the chaise beside her. "You still look a bit pale."

"That's why I'm sitting out here," Kate said, glancing over at Carlotta. "Where's Dad?"

"He had an errand to run." Carlotta looked away, her large pink sunhat flopping in her face as she slurped her own drink. Kate's eyes narrowed in suspicion. This was the second time she'd asked about her father and the second time her mother had given her a vague answer and been unable to look her in the eye. Something was up.

Carlotta changed the subject. "I should have

guessed that Dottie was The Lemur. I knew she was never as senile as she pretended to be, stealing my food."

"It was a great cover, though," Kate said. "We all felt sorry for her. And acting like she needed Alexis to escort her was brilliant. Everyone thought she was a doddering old lady."

"Hmm." From the tone of her mother's voice, Kate imagined her mother rolling her eyes behind those big sunglasses. "And apparently it was Dottie who told Alexis to get her own ride home, not the other way around like Dottie told Sal."

"Yeah, I guess that's why we couldn't find Alexis when we thought she was The Lemur. She'd already left in a taxi."

Carlotta sighed. "I really do hope Alexis didn't know anything about her aunt being The Lemur. I wouldn't want our Benny to get mixed up with her if she did. Word has it he's planning to jet off to Mexico with her for a getaway after the party tonight."

"That's good. Get her away from here and get her mind off things."

Carlotta looked at Kate over the top of her sunglasses. "You really think she didn't know? How dumb is she?"

Kate smirked. Alexis wasn't the brightest, but she

wasn't stupid. Still, Kate felt certain that she'd had no idea what her aunt was up to. "I believe her. Dottie made a career by deceiving people. And we never like to believe bad things about the people we love."

"I guess Benny was right. He swore it couldn't have been Alexis because he was watching her the whole time. Early on from the bridge, and then he was with her when he came down."

"Yeah. He tried to tell us it couldn't be her, but we didn't wait to hear him out."

Carlotta leaned over toward Kate and lowered her voice. "Benny also said Alexis told him she'd written that note Sinclair had, the one inviting him to the storeroom, but that she'd meant it for Benny. She'd thought she'd put it in Benny's pocket when the ship lurched before we set sail, but it had turned out to be Sinclair's suit coat instead." Carlotta snorted.

Kate rolled her eyes. "Right. And Sinclair thought it was me who had slipped it into his pocket and that I wanted to meet him. Not exactly a high-light of the mission for me."

"He was nasty," Gertie said from behind them, where she was putting a flamingo-patterned table-cloth on the long table where they would put all the food later. Carlotta had made a ricotta pie and meatballs, both of which Kate was dying to try. "He tried to grope me when I was cleaning his room."

"He did?" Carlotta cringed.

Gertie turned to look at her. "What? You don't think I'm attractive enough? I might be old, but I've still got it. Anyway, this whole mission was a downer for me. Having to clean. Getting groped. And worst of all, my best painting is at the bottom of the Venice lagoon."

"Yeah, sorry about that. Couldn't be helped. I'm sure you can paint one just as nice. Maybe even better." Kate looked around the poolside. Vic still wasn't here. It was obvious Carlotta wasn't going to tell her where he was, but maybe Gertie would. "Hey, have you seen my father?"

Gertie glanced at Carlotta. "Uh ... no. I haven't, right?"

Kate's suspicions grew, and she leveled a look at her mother.

Carlotta avoided eye contact. "He'll be here soon. But I agree, Gertie, you'll be able to paint one that's even better."

"Maybe. Imagine Dottie stealing paintings at her age. You'd think one would outgrow that kind of behavior." Gertie winked at Carlotta and then turned her attention back to the table. "My money was on that Penny character. I lost fifty bucks to Sal on that bet."

"Oh, speaking of Penny." Carlotta rooted in the navy-blue-striped tote bag beside her chair and pulled out an envelope. "This came for you in today's mail."

Kate opened it and found a get-well card from Wanda Deavers a.k.a Penny Martin. Of course she'd also written that even though Kate had captured The Lemur, Wanda would've discovered the truth herself sooner or later.

Shaking her head, Kate handed the card to her mother to read. "Talk about competitive."

"Yes. Some people never learn." The irony in her mother's voice was not lost on Kate.

"At least you got a look at that hottie boss of yours," Gertie said.

"Actually I didn't."

"What? But he pulled you out of the water and saved you." Gertie laughed. "You should have seen Ace. He was mad as hell. Was gonna jump right in after you. I think he was a little jealous that Max got to save you."

Kate smiled. Her heart warmed thinking that Ace had wanted to save her. And even though Kate had missed her chance to see Max, she'd still caught The

Lemur on her own, and that felt pretty darn good. There would be plenty of chances to see Max later.

Right now she was glad the mission was a success *and* that she didn't have to pretend to be married to Ace Mason anymore. Still, a small part of her had to admit that being fake-married to Ace hadn't been as bad as she'd thought. Except for those stupid pet names. Yeah, she wouldn't miss those. And she was going to enjoy her solo time now that she was in Florida and Ace was back in New York. Hopefully Max wouldn't get any bright ideas about teaming them up again.

Kate relaxed back in her lounge chair and was almost asleep when the gate creaked open. She looked up to see her father clad in a white T-shirt and navy-blue Bermuda shorts dotted with green turtles entering. "Here's Dad now."

Carlotta hopped up from her chair. "Yep. Looks like I need a refill." She ran off toward the bar, leaving Kate staring after her. That was odd.

"Hey, Kitten." Vic stood at the end of the lounge chair, his shadow blocking the sun.

"Hi, Dad. Where have you been?"

"I picked up a little surprise for you."

Kate sat up in her chair. Her father wasn't

holding a bag and he didn't have a present in his hand. "What kind of surprise?"

Vic glanced over at the gate. "Well ..."

Kate followed his gaze to see Ace Mason step through the gate. He wore orange board shorts and a light-blue shirt with a darker stripe down the side. His face blazed into a smile when he met Kate's eyes. He looked good, and Kate would have liked to return the smile, but she had a sinking feeling this meant her solo time was coming to an abrupt end.

Her father shuffled from one foot to the other. "Yeah, Ace is here to help you recuperate. You know, get back on your feet good and solid. That's the surprise."

Kate narrowed her eyes. "Is that so? Whose idea was that?" Clearly Vic was behind this. He'd been trying to get them back together ever since he and Ace had bonded on a previous mission.

Ace stood next to Vic now, looking eager and excited. He pushed her legs gently aside and sat at the end of her chaise.

"It was Max's idea. He gave me the time off to make sure you have a full and speedy recovery." Ace patted her leg. "Isn't that great, Pookie-bear?"

Kate closed her eyes and counted to ten. She contemplated pushing Ace off the end of her chair with her foot, but with that genuine look of hope and caring plastered on his face it would be like kicking a puppy.

Okay, fine. Her alone time was ruined unless she crushed his hopes and sent him away. But somewhere deep down she really didn't want to send him away, so she smiled and said, "Sure. That will be great."

"Good. Max wants to make sure you're in tip-top shape for our next assignment."

Kate's eyes flew open. "*Our* next assignment?"

"Yeah. Didn't he tell you?" Ace raised a brow at the look on her face. "Guess not. Okay, well he said he'd text. He'll probably do it later today. I don't know much about it, just that it will be one of your most important assignments yet and we'll have to work very closely. He said we proved to be a great team on The Lemur mission. Won't that be great?"

Kate leaned back with a sigh and sipped her drink. Maybe it wouldn't be so bad to work with a partner on the next one. And she and Ace had always worked well together in the past. And next time she'd have nothing to prove. She'd already proven herself by catching The Lemur. If Max wanted her to work with Ace on the next case, so be it. After all, what could possibly go wrong?

****

Join my email list and receive emails about my latest book releases - don't miss out on early release discounts:
http://www.leighanndobbs.com/newsletter

If you want to receive a text message on your cell phone for new releases, text COZYMYSTERY to 88202 (sorry, this only works for US cell phones!)

Join my Facebook Readers group and get special content and the inside scoop on my books:
https://www.facebook.com/groups/ldobbsreaders

Other Books in This series:

Hidden Agemda (Book 1)
Ancient Hiss Story (Book 2)

Also by Leighann Dobbs

Cozy Mysteries

Kate Diamond Mystery Adventures

***

Hidden Agemda (Book 1)

Ancient Hiss Story (Book 2)

Heist Society (Book 3)

Silver Hollow

Paranormal Cozy Mystery Series

***

A Spell of Trouble (Book 1)

Spell Disaster (Book 2)

Nothing to Croak About (Book 3)

Cry Wolf (Book 4)

Mooseamuck Island Cozy Mystery Series

* * *

A Zen For Murder

A Crabby Killer

A Treacherous Treasure

Mystic Notch

Cat Cozy Mystery Series

* * *

Ghostly Paws

A Spirited Tail

A Mew To A Kill

Paws and Effect

Probable Paws

Blackmoore Sisters

Cozy Mystery Series

* * *

Dead Wrong

Dead & Buried

Dead Tide

Buried Secrets

Deadly Intentions

A Grave Mistake

Spell Found

Fatal Fortune

Lexy Baker Cozy Mystery Series

* * *

Lexy Baker Cozy Mystery Series Boxed Set Vol 1 (Books 1-4)

Or buy the books separately:

Killer Cupcakes

Dying For Danish

Murder, Money and Marzipan

3 Bodies and a Biscotti

Brownies, Bodies & Bad Guys

Bake, Battle & Roll

Wedded Blintz

Scones, Skulls & Scams

Ice Cream Murder

Mummified Meringues

Brutal Brulee (Novella)

No Scone Unturned

Cream Puff Killer

Hazel Martin Historical Mystery Series

***

Murder at Lowry House (book 1)

Murder by Misunderstanding (book 2)

Regency Matchmaker Mysteries

***

An Invitation to Murder (Book 1)

The Baffling Burglaries of Bath (Book 2)

Reluctant Romance

Sweet Romance (Written As Annie Dobbs)

Firefly Inn Series

***

Another Chance (Book 1)

Another Wish (Book 2)

Hometown Hearts Series

***

No Getting Over You (Book 1)

A Change of Heart (Book 2)

Kate Diamond Mystery Adventure Series

Hidden Agemda (book 1)

Ancient Hiss Story (book 2)

***

Sweetrock Sweet and Spicy Cowboy Romance

Some Like It Hot

Too Close For Comfort

———

Regency Romance

* * *

Scandals and Spies Series:

Kissing The Enemy

Deceiving the Duke

Tempting the Rival

Charming the Spy

Pursuing the Traitor

Captivating the Captain

The Unexpected Series:

An Unexpected Proposal

An Unexpected Passion

Dobbs Fancytales:

Dobbs Fancytales Boxed Set Collection

———

Western Historical Romance

***

Goldwater Creek Mail Order Brides:

Faith

American Mail Order Brides Series:

Chevonne: Bride of Oklahoma

————————

Magical Romance with a Touch of Mystery

***

Something Magical

Curiously Enchanted

ROMANTIC SUSPENSE

WRITING AS LEE ANNE JONES:

***

The Rockford Security Series:

About the Author

USA Today Bestselling author Leighann Dobbs has had a passion for reading since she was old enough to hold a book, but she didn't put pen to paper until much later in life. After a twenty-year career as a software engineer with a few side trips into selling antiques and making jewelry, she realized you can't make a living reading books, so she tried her hand at writing them and discovered she had a passion for that, too! She lives in New Hampshire with her husband, Bruce, their trusty Chihuahua mix, Mojo, and beautiful rescue cat, Kitty.

Her book "Dead Wrong" won the "Best Mystery Romance" award at the 2014 Indie Romance Convention.

Her book "Ghostly Paws" was the 2015 Chanticleer Mystery & Mayhem First Place category winner in the Animal Mystery category.

Don't miss out on the early buyers discount on

Leighann's next cozy mystery - signup for email notifications:

http://www.leighanndobbs.com/newsletter

Want text alerts for new releases? TEXT alert straight on your cellphone. Just text COZYMYS-TERY to 88202

(sorry, this only works for US cell phones!)

Connect with Leighann on Facebook:

http://facebook.com/leighanndobbsbooks

Join her VIP Readers group on Facebook:

https://www.facebook.com/groups/ldobbsreaders

Made in the USA
Lexington, KY
27 June 2018